THE GUNSMITH

438

The Treasure of Little Bighorn

Books by J.R. Roberts
(Robert J. Randisi)

The Gunsmith series
Books 1 - 225

The Lady Gunsmith series
Books 1 - 5

Angel Eyes series
Books 1 - 4

Tracker series
Books 1 - 4

Mountain Jack Pike series
Books 1 - 4

COMING SOON!

The Gunsmith
439 – Blackbeard's Gun

For more information visit:
www.speakingvolumes.us

THE GUNSMITH

438

The Treasure of Little Bighorn

J.R. Roberts

SPEAKING VOLUMES, LLC
NAPLES, FLORIDA
2018

The Treasure of Little Bighorn

ISBN 978-1-62815-863-2

Prologue

The Bighorn River, June 1876

Captain Grant Marsh squinted into the dark distance. While riverboat captains normally employed pilots on their boats, Marsh always preferred to pilot his steamship, the Far West, on his own, when he could. He was doing that this night, while traveling the Bighorn River.

Grant Marsh looked like a riverboat captain. He was tall, barrel-chested, in his 50s with grey hair and beard, and usually had a pipe in his mouth. He didn't strive to look like a riverboat captain, he just did.

On this dark night he was in the pilothouse alone, having given his pilot some time off. It was generally known that Marsh was on a mission to bring Lt. Colonel George Armstrong Custer and his men supplies and ammunition, with which to battle Crazy Horse and his Lakota Sioux warriors. What was not generally known was that there was also $375,000 in gold bars in the hold of the ship, which Marsh had acquired from miners who had worked long and hard digging the valued substance out of the ground. Hopefully, with no one aware of that part of his cargo, there would be no robbery attempts, as often occurred on these waters. He had only one more stop before reaching the shores of the Little Bighorn river on the Crow reservation, where he would offload Custer's cargo, which was valued more than gold to the Colonel and his men.

The largest port before they would leave the Bighorn to travel along its tributary, the Little Bighorn, was in Graybull, Wyoming. By first light they would be pulling in there so some passengers could disembark and certain items could be unloaded. After that they would have no passengers, just the job they'd been hired to do.

The U.S. Army had leased the 190 foot boat to use as headquarters at the mouth of the upper Missouri River, for the duration of the 1876 campaign against the Sioux and Cheyenne. The Far West drew only 20 inches of water, which meant it could get close enough to be accessible from shore. From there they planned their attack on a Sioux settlement along the banks of the Little Bighorn River.

***

When they arrived and dropped anchor, there was no reason whatsoever for the Army to know what was in the hold of the ship. The gold was safe until this job was over and Captain Marsh could get it unloaded and stowed away safely.

With the boat moored the Captain and his crew were largely free to do whatever they pleased. They were, after all, not part of the U.S. Army, just independent contractors. In fact, they spent quite a bit of time a mile or so away from the ship, fishing to their heart's content.

***

On June 29th Captain Marsh was doing just that, standing on shore with several of his men. They had to fish away from the activity on the ship, which would frighten the brown trout away.

"Captain?" the first mate, Rushmore Billings, said. He was known to the Captain and the crew as "Rush."

"Yeah?"

"Rider comin'."

They all turned, touched the pistols they had tucked into their belts. But the rider was what they had come to know as a "tame" Indian, used by the Army as a scout.

"I wonder what he wants?" Eddie Lee asked.

"Shut up, Eddie," Rush said.

"Let's find out," Marsh said.

They put their poles down and moved to intercept the rider. The Indian dismounted and, unable to speak English, made himself understood through sign language and drawing on the ground.

"Custer's dead," Rush said.

"Jesus!" Marsh breathed.

"What the hell—" Eddie Lee said.

***

Later they were addressed by the commanding officer, Captain Everett Dobbs.

"You no longer have to deliver guns and ammunition," the Captain said, "you're on a mission of mercy to pick up and transport survivors—if there are any. It doesn't sound good."

Lt. Colonel George Armstrong Custer's 7th Calvary regiment had been besieged and decimated by the Lakota, Cheyenne and Arapaho tribes, led by Chief Crazy Horse and Chief Gall. Marsh was asked to make room on his boat for surviving casualties.

"Okay," Marsh said to the clerk, "thanks."

The Captain went back down the gang plank.

"Rush!"

"Yessir?"

"Unload the rest of the guns and ammunition that was meant for the 7th Calvary."

"Sir?"

"They won't be needing it, anymore. We need the room for casualties."

"Yessir." Rush moved closer and lowered his voice. "And the, other cargo?"

"Yes, we'll need to unload that, too, but not here," Marsh said. "Somewhere . . . secluded."

"Yessir."

"Rush, what do we gotta do with—" Eddie Lee started.

"Shut up, Eddie."

While the crew unloaded the munitions that had been meant for Custer, Captain Grant Marsh went over, in his head, the route they would be taking back to Graybull. He had to pick out a secluded spot along the way, not too close to shore but not so secluded that they would not be able to go back and find $375,000 worth of gold bars. And then he had to hope against all hope that when they did go back, the gold would still be there. After all, not only would Marsh and Rush know where the gold was, but certain crew members, as well. And while Marsh trusted his mate and crew—well, $375,000 *was,* after all, $375,000.

Of course, there was always the possibility that there wouldn't be *too* many casualties, that way the Far West would not be able to carry them plus the gold. In that case, he wouldn't have to let the gold bars out of his sight. So it was up to Captain Marsh if he wanted to take the risk of carrying both.

Too much weight would certainly sink the Far West, but $375,000 was, after all, $375,000.

Certainly worth the risk, wasn't it?

The ship had to enter the Little Bighorn River to pick up the 54 survivors of the Little Bighorn Massacre.

"We're ridin' low, Captain."

"I know," Marsh said.

"We're gonna have to—"

"I know!"

"So, where should we, uh, unloaded the cargo?"

"Let's wait and see, Rush," Captain Marsh said, "let's wait and see."

Chapter One

Initially, Clint Adams knew nothing of the lost Treasure of Little Bighorn, as some had come to call it. He did, however, personally know George Armstrong Custer, and was not the least bit surprised that Custer had been outflanked, out maneuvered and outfought by Crazy Horse and Gall—especially since a lot of what they employed had been learned from the great Sitting Bull. In effect, Custer had been defeated by the combined force of 3 great Indian minds.

But that was in the past, and Clint did not devote any time to dredging it up if he didn't have to. After all, he may have known Custer, but they were far from friends. In addition, he'd never had an iota of respect for the man.

So when his friend, Artie Small, said to him, "You remember Custer and the Little Bighorn, right?"

Clint stared back at the man and asked, "What about them?"

Artie smiled . . .

***

Artie Small was a big man.

When they first met, Clint made the mistake of laughing when Artie was introduced. Artie beat him to a pulp, and they'd been friends ever since. That was five years ago, in Abilene. Since then had seen each other perhaps half a dozen times, everywhere from Mexico to Alaska. Artie Small traveled far and wide, looking for the big strike.

"This time," he said to Clint, "I think I got it."

"You always say that, Artie," Clint reminded him.

"Look," Artie said, "what are you doin' in Riverton?"

"Just passing through."

"And you don't believe in coincidences, right?"

"Right."

"So the fact that I saw you on the street here, and that we're sittin' in this restaurant havin' steaks, ain't a coincidence," Artie said. "We was supposed to meet here."

"Why?"

"Because I need a stake, Clint," Artie said, "and I need a partner."

"To do what?"

Artie looked around to make sure nobody could overhear them. The surrounding tables nearest them in the small café were empty. The occupied tables were too far away.

"You ever heard of the treasure of the Little Bighorn?" he asked Clint.

"I may have heard it mentioned," Clint said, "but nothing specific."

"You ever heard of Captain Grant Marsh and the Far West steamboat?"

"No."

"Well," Artie said, "I'm gonna tell you a story . . ."

***

After Artie had finished telling Clint about Captain Grant Marsh and his $375,000 worth of gold bars he sat back and popped the last hunk of his steak into his mouth.

Clint had finished his own while Artie was talking, and now he poured himself another cup of coffee.

Artie chewed, swallowed, and asked, "So, whataya think?"

"Is this another one of your hair-brained schemes, Artie?" Clint asked.

"Ain't nothin' hair-brained about this, Clint, whatever that means."

"It means—"

"—I can guess what it means!" Artie said. "Look, that fella you know in Texas, what's his name?"

"Rick? In Labyrinth?"

"Yeah, him," Artie said, "You say he knows everythin', right?"

"Pretty much."

"Okay, then send him a telegram. Ask him if he knows anythin' about Captain Marsh—but don't mention a treasure. We don't want some big mouth telegraph operator spreadin' the word."

"Okay."

"If your friend Rick says I'm on the level, then you stake me, be my partner, and I'll split with you fifty-fifty."

"Just the two of us?" Clint asked. "How would we operate a boat big enough to carry that much gold?"

"I got a plan," Artie said, "but I ain't gonna tell ya unless you're in."

"Fair enough. But this isn't one of your—"

"—no, it ain't a hair-brained plan!"

"Okay, okay."

"Jesus, what is that anyway?" Artie asked. "'Hair-brained?' Where did that even come from?"

"To tell you the truth, I don't know," Clint said. "It's just a saying."

"Well, if you don't know where it came from, stop sayin' it, all right?"

"Deal," Clint said.

Chapter Two

Rick Hartman owned the saloon Rick's Place in Labyrinth, Texas, and he pretty much never left there. But he had ears all over the country—and further—and information was coming in to him all the time. If anyone would know about Captain Grant Marsh, it would be him.

So Clint agreed to send a telegram to Rick, and then meet up with Artie Small again when he got a reply.

They left the Riverton café and went their separate ways. Artie said he still had work to do to get ready to go after the treasure.

"That is," he added, "if you decide not to partner up with me."

"So you've got other options?" Clint asked.

"Maybe a couple," Artie said, "but nobody I'd trust like I trust you."

Clint headed for the telegraph office, went inside and wrote out his message to Rick, handed it to the clerk. Of course, the man had to read it first. He didn't seem to react when he saw the name, Captain Grant Marsh. He simply counted the words, charged Clint, and then sent it.

"Where will ya be when the answer comes back?" the man asked.

"Right here," Clint said, pointing to a nearby bench.

"You're gonna wait?"

"I've got nothing else to do." He also knew that Rick Hartman would have the telegram in his hands just moments after it was sent. The reply would not be long in coming.

"Suit yerself," the clerk said, with a shrug.

Clint sat on the bench and listened to the click-click-click of the key as the clerk sent the telegram.

The answer came back in ten minutes. The clerk seemed surprised, but hurriedly sat and took it down, then passed it over to Clint.

"Thank you," Clint said.

He took it outside with him before reading it. According to Rick, he knew who Captain Marsh was and it might be worth Clint's time to pursue the matter. Nothing was said about gold or treasure, but Clint read behind the lines about it being "worth his while."

He went in search of Artie Small. It wasn't hard to find a man as big as Artie in a small river town like Riverton.

***

They went to a small saloon, got two beers and a table in the back.

Clint said, "All right, tell me more."

"The story goes Captain Grant Marsh tried to pick up the survivors of the Little Bighorn battle, about fifty of them, without unloading his gold bars. But on the way back downriver his boat, the Far West, was in danger of sinking. He had no choice but to unload."

"And did everyone on board know about the gold?" Clint asked. "Even the surviving soldiers?"

"No," Small said, "not according to what I heard. Only the Captain, his first mate, and a few key members of his crew knew what was in the crates. They ferried them to shore and buried them."

"And?"

"And that's it."

"What happened when they went back to get the gold?" Clint asked.

"According to the story," Small said, "they never did. The gold is still buried on the shore of the Little Bighorn River, somewhere."

"How much of it?"

"Three hundred and seventy-five thousand dollars worth," Small said. "That was eighteen seventy-six. I don't know how the price of gold has changed since then. Could be worth more, or less. But even less is good."

"And how do you intend to get the gold and transport it to . . . where do you intend to transport it to?"

"First things first," Artie Small said. "We gotta find it."

"You don't know where it is?"

"I told you," Small said, "buried somewhere along the Little Bighorn River."

"And how far does the Little Bighorn stretch?"

"It's about a hundred and thirty miles from Graybull to Hardin."

"So you're going to search a hundred and thirty miles of shoreline?"

"No, of course not."

"Well, that's a relief."

"We can narrow it down."

"And how do we do that?"

Artie Small looked around to be sure nobody was listening.

"I have a man who was on the boat when the gold was offloaded."

"He knew about the gold?"

"He did."

"How?"

"He heard some talk."

"So he knows where it's buried?"

Artie Small winced. "He has an idea."

"An idea?" Clint asked. "You said you had it narrowed down."

"I do," Small said.

"How narrowed down?"

Artie Small winced again and said, "Fifty miles . . . or so?"

Chapter Three

Clint wasn't convinced.

"Have you ever been to Little Bighorn country?" he asked Artie Small.

"No, I haven't," Small said. "That's why I recruited Eddie Lee."

"This is the man who was on the boat?"

"That's right," Small said. "He was one of the deck hands."

"Then does he know what happened to the Captain and the boat after they delivered the survivors to safety?"

"No," Small said. "He says when they got back to Graybull, Captain Grant and the first mate, Rush Billings—"

"Rush?"

"His name was Rushmore, but Eddie said they all called him Rush."

"Yeah, okay."

"The Captain and the first mate let a lot of the deck hands go, including Eddie."

"So what happened to the Far West?"

"Nobody seems to know."

"Well, maybe Captain Marsh took it back up the Little Bighorn and collected the gold."

"Eddie says no."

"How does he know?"

"He's been in touch with some of the other deck hands from that time," Small said. "The word is Captain Marsh disappeared."

"Do they think maybe the first mate killed him?" Clint asked. "He could've done that, and then gone back for the gold, himself."

"No, he couldn't."

"Why not?"

"Because he *is* dead. That's somethin' everybody I talked to agrees on."

"How did he die?"

"I ain't sure, but maybe Eddie knows."

"And where's Eddie?"

"He's gonna meet us in Thermopolis."

"Thermopolis is further south on the Bighorn than Graybull," Clint pointed out. "Why not meet in Graybull?"

"Eddie's in Thermopolis gettin' us a boat."

"What kind of boat?"

"I ain't sure."

"We can't handle a steamboat, or an old paddleboat," Clint said. "Not without a full crew."

"No, nothin' like that," Small said, "but Eddie says he'll get somethin' big enough for us."

"And for the gold?"

"And for the gold."

"Hey Artie, how much of a cut is Eddie in for?" Clint asked.

Artie Small hesitated, then said, "Oh, uh, about twenty-five percent."

"About?"

Small nodded. "Twenty percent."

"So when you and I go half-and-half," Clint figured, "you actually mean I'm getting fifty percent of eighty percent, right?"

"Right."

"So that's a hundred and fifty thousand for each of us, and seventy-five thousand for him."

"It is?"

"You didn't do the math, Artie, when you agreed to give him twenty-five percent?"

"I ain't so good at sums, Clint," Artie Small said. "You know that. Not like you. Look how ya did that in yer head just now."

"Is there anybody else in for a cut?" Clint asked.

"No, just the three of us."

Over the years, in his travels, Clint had invested in many businesses, including some mines. The money he collected from his partners went into the bank. At the moment he had a healthy bank account, but after all, $150,000 was $150,000.

"Are you in?" Artie Small asked.

"I tell you what, Artie," Clint said. "I'm in as far as Thermopolis. I want to meet and talk to this Eddie Lee, myself get his measure."

"Hey, no problem," Small said. "But, uh, to get to Thermopolis . . ."

"What?"

"I kinda need a horse."

"So buy one."

Artie winced. He did that a lot. It wasn't usually followed by good news.

"I kinda don't have any money."

"Must be why you were so glad to run into me here in Riverton."

"Aw, come on," Artie Small said. "We're friends, Clint. I was glad to see ya—"

"I know, I know," Clint said. "No problem, I'll buy you a horse."

"Great! Thanks."

"You can pay me back out of your share."

"Oh, yeah," Artie said. "Sure."

"We might as well go and get it now," Clint said.

Chapter Four

The livery where Clint had boarded Eclipse also had some horses for rent and sale. He walked over there with Artie Small and picked out a horse.

"What about that one?" Artie asked.

"Too small, Artie," Clint said. "You need a horse that can abide your bulk, and the distance."

"Like that one?" Artie pointed to a large grey gelding.

"Just like that one," Clint said.

"Okay, fine," Artie said. "Why don't you talk to the owner, here."

"Don't you want to be in on the negotiations?" Clint asked. "After all, you're going to have to pay me back."

"That's okay," Artie said. "I trust you, Clint. I know you'll get a good deal."

"And what are you going to do?"

"I'll get us some supplies," Artie said.

"It's only about sixty miles from here to Thermopolis, Artie."

"Right," Artie said, "Supplies for one night. I'll see you later."

The big man left the stable and Clint went to find the owner to make the deal.

After examining the gelding, finding that he was a sound 6 year old, Clint made the deal with Vern, the hostler. Then he bought a saddle and bridle. All of that done he took the gelding out of the corral and put him in a stall next to Eclipse.

"You two boys get acquainted," he said. "You'll probably be partners for a while."

Clint never referred to horses as "it" but rather "he" or "she." They had personalities to him, especially his own, Duke and Eclipse. He'd had other mounts in his life, but those two stood out.

He left the livery and walked over to the saloon, where he found Artie Small leaning on the bar. When the big man saw him, he raised his mug.

"Make that deal, didja?" Artie asked.

"I did," Clint said. "You're all set for a horse."

"Great."

"What about supplies?"

"We can pick 'em up in the mornin', on the way out of town."

"So we're leaving tomorrow?"

"Why waste time?" Artie asked. "You want a beer?"

"Sure."

"Just so you know," Artie said, "I don't, uh—"

"Yeah, I know," Clint said. "I've got it."

He paid for the beer Artie had already consumed, and then two more.

The saloon began to get busier around them, so they took their next beers to a table, one from which Clint would be able to see the whole room.

"I'm kind of concerned over what kind of boat this fella Eddie Lee is going to get us," Clint said.

"Eddie's a river rat, Clint," Artie said. "He'll get us what we need."

"Well, since I'm footing the bill, I think I should be consulted. I'm not looking forward to buying a paddle-boat of my own."

"It'll most likely be a barge, or a flat-bottomed boat. I don't expect that we'll be able to transport all the gold bars at one time. That means when we find 'em some will go on the boat, and we'll have to hide the rest, again. Someplace different, naturally, so nobody else finds 'em."

"And do we know for sure that there are others looking for the gold?"

"It's a hidden treasure, Clint," Artie said, "and where you've got treasure, you've got a treasure hunt."

"So we're not the only ones looking."

"No," Artie said, "but we're the only ones who have a crewman from the Far West workin' with us to find it . . . I think."

"You think?"

"Well, Eddie said he's seen some men he used to work with," Artie said. "You know, others from the Far West."

"How many others?" Clint asked. "And who?"

"Well, he ain't seen the captain or the first mate, if that's what you're thinkin'."

"How many has he seen, Artie?"

"A few."

"Why do I get the feeling there's something you're not telling me, Artie."

"Like what?"

"Like we're in some kind of a race to find this gold?" Clint asked.

"Not a race, exactly," Artie said, "but there are others. After all, we're talkin' about gold, ain't we?"

"Yes, we are, Artie," Clint agreed, "we're talking about gold."

Chapter Five

"We're also talking about you not telling me the whole truth," Clint added.

"Okay, look," Artie said, "the word's gotten around about this treasure. I *was* working with a partner, but he decided to leave me behind and go his own way."

"What partner?" Clint asked.

"Nobody you know," Artie said. "His name is Cassidy Polk, and he's a lying, cheatin', connivin' sonofabitch."

"Excuse me for saying so, Artie," Clint said, "but so are you, sometimes."

"Yeah, maybe," Artie said, "but not this time. This time I'm the victim. We collected all our information together, and then he took off with a coupla friends of his and left me behind. Well, if he thinks he's gonna find that treasure before me, he's gonna find out how wrong he is." Artie reached across the table and clasped Clint left wrist in a vicelike grip. "I just need you to help me do that, Clint."

"And for that I get my fifty-percent," Clint said.

"Right."

"And I foot the bill."

"Just in the beginning," Artie said. "Like I said, I just need a stake. I had some money, but that bastard Cass Polk took it with him."

"So you're recruiting me for my gun?" Clint asked.

"Whataya take me for?" Artie asked. "I know you don't hire out your gun. Look, my partner turned on me, and I need a new one. And here you are, in Riverton, where I'm stuck. I know you don't believe in coincidences, but this could be fate."

To Clint "fate" was just a shorter word for "coincidence."

"Okay," Clint said, "my offer still stands. I'm your partner until we get to Thermopolis and I talk to Eddie Lee. If there's anything about him I don't like, I'm out."

"Eddie's a good guy," Artie said. "You'll see."

"Let's finish these and turn in. If we get an early start, we might be able to make the whole ride in one day."

"Whatever you say!"

***

They left the saloon and headed back to the hotel they were both staying in. Artie Small called that a coincidence, too. To Clint, it was simply the cleanest place he had found in town.

"Wait! What's that?" Artie asked, as they approached the hotel.

It was late, the street was empty except for them.

"What?" Clint asked.

"Listen."

He did. It was dead quiet.

"I don't hear a thing."

"I thought somebody was followin' us."

"If they were, I'd know," Clint told him, as they started walking again. "You're just jumpy."

"Treasure hunters, Clint," Artie said. "They ain''t above shootin' you in the back."

"Well, that's not going to happen tonight, Artie," Clint assured him.

They reached the hotel lobby in safety and each went to their room after agreeing they'd leave early.

"Can't be at first light, though," Artie said. "Gotta wait for the general store to open so we can get our supplies."

"Okay," Clint said. "We'll have breakfast first, then stop in for the supplies as soon as they open the door."

"I'll see ya then," Artie said. "And Clint, thanks for comin' on board."

Clint went to his own room, thinking that he wasn't completely on board, yet. First he would have to see what kind of boat he was agreeing to board.

***

In the morning they had breakfast at a small restaurant across the street from the General Store. As soon as they saw the door open they paid their bill and walked across, leading their horses.

Artie had brought coffee, jerky, and some canned peaches. They split the supplies between their saddlebags, and then mounted up. Artie's gelding, though large, was not as big as Clint's Darley Arabian, but since Artie Small sat tall in the saddle, they were pretty much on even terms.

"Ready to move out?" Clint asked.

"Thermopolis, it is," Artie said. He looked nervous, his eyes darting about.

"What's wrong?" Clint asked.

Artie looked at him.

"Somethin' still doesn't feel right."

"Okay, then," Clint said, never one to completely dismiss someone else's instincts, "we'll keep our eyes out for back-shooting treasure hunters."

"That sounds good, Clint," Artie said. "That sounds real good."

***

Artie Small wanted to push on and get to Thermopolis that night, but Clint insisted they camp and ride in come morning.

"Your horse needs a rest," he added. "He can't keep up with Eclipse."

"It's fine," Artie said. "It can make it."

"He," Clint insisted, "needs to rest. Besides, if you're still worried about back-shooting treasure hunters, the dark certainly gives them an advantage."

"Yeah, okay," Artie said, finally. "You know best, Clint."

"When it comes to back-shooters I do."

They made camp about ten miles outside of Thermopolis. In the morning it would be an easy ride to get into town before noon.

Clint took care of the horse while Artie started the fire and the coffee. When Clint was done he walked over and accepted a cup from the big man.

"Care for some peaches?" Artie asked.

"Just some jerky," Clint said. "That should do it."

Artie passed the beef jerky over to Clint, then opened a can of peaches for himself.

"I love these," he said, "especially the syrup."

"You said Lee will already be there when we get to town?" Clint asked.

"Eddie should be there and have our boat ready," Artie responded.

"I hope he knows what he's doing," Clint said.

"I told you," Artie said, "he's an experienced river rat, he was on the Far West, and knows the Little Bighorn river."

"But he doesn't know the exact spot the gold was hidden."

"No," Artie said, "but he thinks he'll know it when he sees it."

"Then why doesn't he just go and get it?"

"Because nobody can do it alone," Artie said. "Nobody can bring the gold back brick by brick. And nobody can fight alone, if it comes to a fight. That's why he threw in with me and Polk."

"And now you and me."

"Well," Artie said, "when we get there I'll introduce him to you."

"Are you sure he'll accept me?"

"He's gotta," Artie said, "'cause we can't do this without you."

"He was there first, Artie," Clint pointed out. "If he doesn't want me in, I'm out."

"Don't worry," Artie said. "He'll want you in. You got my word on that."

Chapter Six

They rode into Thermopolis well before noon. It was a busy river town, boats coming and going, using its docks and warehouses. But they directed their horses away from the river for now, choosing instead to board them in the center of town, away from the activity on the water.

"Eddie knows Thermopolis," Artie told Clint. "He said to get a room at the Paddleboat Hotel.

"The Paddleboat."

"Yup."

So they walked from the livery, keeping their eyes open and finally asking somebody where the Paddleboat Hotel was.

The man they asked laughed at first, then stared at them and said, "Oh, you're serious."

"We're meetin' a friend there," Artie said.

"Oh, well, it's right next to the Paddleboat Saloon, on Rust street."

"Rust?" Clint said. "There's a street called Rust?"

The man nodded and said, "That's where you'll find the Paddleboat. Good luck."

"Good luck?" Clint repeated, looking at Artie.

"I'm sure it's fine," he said. "Eddie wouldn't have told us to meet him there if it was so bad."

"Let's find out."

***

Following the man's directions they found their way to Rust Street. Clint thought the appearance of the street was very fitting. There was refuse along the way, two legged and otherwise, and the buildings looked like they were going to collapse any minute.

When they reached the Paddleboat Saloon and the Hotel they stopped and stared.

"Not so bad, huh?" Clint asked, sarcastically.

"Might be better than it looks," Artie said.

"Just don't sneeze while we're inside," Clint said. "It might bring it down around us."

They entered the hotel lobby which, oddly enough, looked much better than the outside.

"I think I see where they're spending their money," Clint said. "I wonder how the rooms look."

"I guess we'll find out," Artie said.

They went to the front desk, where a young clerk smiled at them.

"Welcome to the Paddleboat," he said. "Can I help you?"

"We're lookin' for a friend of ours," Artie said. "Ed Lee."

"Ed . . . Lee?" the clerk asked.

"Eddie," Artie said. "Yeah."

"Yes, I think he has a room here," the clerk said, looking at the book. "Yes, room six, upstairs."

"Is he there now?" Artie asked.

"No, he's not in, uh, now."

"Can we get rooms?" Clint asked.

"Rooms?" Artie asked him.

"Yes, one each."

"We have two rooms," the clerk said.

"Nothing overlooking the street," Clint said.

"Right, three and four?"

"Sounds good."

The young man handed them their keys while they signed the register.

"When Mr. Lee comes in," Clint said, "would you tell him we're here?"

"Um, sure," he said, "if Mr. Lee comes in I'll, uh, tell him."

They went upstairs and, as they passed room 6, Clint stopped.

"What is it?" Artie asked.

"I've got a bad feeling," Clint said.

Chapter Seven

When the knock came at Clint's door he hoped it was Artie Small. It wasn't. It was a tall man in his 30s, wearing a badge.

"Mr. Adams?"

"Yes."

"Clint Adams, the Gunsmith?"

"That's right."

"I'm Sheriff Glen Dayton," the man said. "I understand you were looking for an Edward Lee here at the hotel?"

"That's right, I am."

"Well then, maybe you should come with me."

"Why? What's it about?" Clint asked.

"It's about your friend."

"He's not actually my friend."

"But . . . you said you were looking for him," the lawman said.

"Well, I am, but the man I'm here with is his friend, not me."

"Oh, and who would that be?"

"His name's Artie Small," Clint said. "He's in room four."

"Well then," the sheriff said, "I suppose we'd better get him, too."

"And go where?"

"You'll see."

Clint had answered the door with his gun in hand. Now he holstered it, took the holster off the bedpost and strapped it on, then went out into the hall with the sheriff.

They walked down the hall and knocked on Artie Small's door. When the big man opened it, the sheriff looked up at him, somewhat surprised.

"Artie, the sheriff says he has something to show us," Clint said. "It has to do with Eddie Lee."

"Oh, shit," Artie said. "Did he get himself arrested?"

The sheriff didn't answer.

"He wants to show us," Clint said.

"Okay," Artie said, since he was fully dressed. "Let's go."

The sheriff led them out of the hotel and down a few blocks until they reached an undertaker's office.

"Oh Christ," Artie said.

He and Clint followed the sheriff inside, where they were met by a small man who looked like a store clerk.

"This is Upton, the undertaker around here," the sheriff said. "Upton, show these fellas your newest guest."

"Yes, sir. This way."

The man led Clint and Artie to a back room, where a dead man was lying on a table.

"Is that him?" Clint asked.

"That's him," Artie said. "Damn it, that's Eddie Lee."

Clint turned to the undertaker.

"When did this happen?"

"Yesterday."

"We missed him by a day," Artie said. "Shit."

They left the back room, found the sheriff still waiting for them.

"Is that your friend?" the lawman asked.

"That's him," Artie said.

"What was he doin' here in town?" Sheriff Dayton asked.

"He was supposed to be buyin' us a boat," Artie said.

"What kind of boat?" Dayton asked.

"Oh . . ."

"A small one," Clint said, "that three men could handle. How was he killed?"

"He was shot," Dayton said.

"Where?"

"Right on the street," the lawman said. "Drygulched. Nobody saw who shot him."

"Or they're not saying," Clint added.

"Right. You fellas wouldn't have some idea of who shot him, wouldja?"

"No," Clint said.

"Not me," Artie said. "Eddie was a nice guy. Don't know why anybody would wanna shoot him."

"How'd you know someone would come looking for him, Sheriff?" Clint asked.

"Oh, I just put the word out at some of the hotels, in case anybody asked. Guess I got lucky."

"Luckier than him," Clint said.

"Will you fellas pay to bury him?"

Artie looked at Clint.

"Okay, yes," Clint said. "I'll pay."

"Then I'll leave you to make arrangements with Upton," Dayton said.

"I suppose I'll end up paying his hotel bill, too," Clint said to Artie.

"I wonder what the hell he was doing that got him shot?" Artie said. "I just hope it wasn't . . ." He lowered his voice. ". . . you know."

The sheriff didn't hear that last part, but he heard enough.

"You might want to ask the woman he was with," the lawman said, "I haven't been able to get anythin' out of her."

As the sheriff walked out Artie looked at Clint.

"Woman?"

Chapter Eight

Clint paid the undertaker to bury Eddie Lee, and then the man gave them the dead man's possessions, which weren't much.

Clint and Artie left the undertaker and started walking back to the hotel.

"If Eddie Lee had a woman," Artie said, "where would she be?"

"Probably in his room," Clint said.

"Oh, I don't think he'd have a woman in that way."

"Then in what way?"

"They were probably partners."

"He was going to bring a woman in on this?" Clint asked.

"I brought you in," Artie pointed out. "Maybe she was backin' him."

"So you got money from me, and he got money from her?" Clint said.

"That makes more sense than her bein' his woman," Artie said. "I mean, you saw him lying on that slab. He was an ugly little guy."

"Yeah, I guess he was. But we better check his room, anyway."

"Okay."

When they got back to the hotel they started for the stairs, but then Clint said, "Wait a minute." He walked to the front desk.

"Sir?" the clerk said, nervously.

"Why didn't you tell us the man we were looking for was dead?" Clint asked.

"Um, the sheriff just said I should tell him if anyone asked for him," the clerk said. "I'm sorry, sir, but—"

"Never mind," Clint said. "Is there a woman staying in Lee's room?"

"No, sir."

"Okay, thanks."

Before Clint could join Artie, who was waiting at the foot of the stairs, the clerk stopped him.

"Sir?"

"Yes?"

"The woman has her own room," he said. "Room number one."

"Thank you."

"You're welcome, sir," the clerk said. "Anything else I can do . . ."

Clint joined Artie at the stairs.

"Room one," he said. "Let's go."

They went up the stairs and knocked on the door. When the woman answered they were both surprised. She was a stunning, auburn-haired beauty who obviously would not be interested in Eddie Lee in "that way." For one thing, she as almost six feet tall.

Or so they thought.

She pointed at Artie and said, "You'd be Artie Small."

"That's right."

"Eddie told me about you," she said. "But not about you." She looked at Clint.

"I'm Clint Adams."

"*The* Clint Adams?" she asked.

"The only one I know of," Clint said.

"So, the Gunsmith, right?"

"Right."

"Hey," she said, smiling for the first time, "I didn't know you were part of this."

"And we didn't know about you," Clint said. "Uh, what's your name?"

"Oh," she said, "I'm Fiona."

"Fiona," Artie said.

"When did you two get here?" she asked.

"Just a little while ago."

"So did you hear about Eddie?"

"We did," Clint said, "the sheriff told us."

"It was too bad," she said. "Things were goin' so well."

"Were they?" Clint asked. "Maybe we could go somewhere and you could tell us about that."

"Sure," she said. "How about next door?"

Chapter Nine

The Paddleboat Saloon wasn't busy, and they were able to get a table of their choice. A tired looking saloon girl came over and took their order for three beers. Or maybe she just looked tired compared to Fiona, who seemed to be all energy.

"It was awful," she said. "According to the sheriff somebody just shot him down in the street. Why would they do something like that?"

"Treasure," Artie said.

"Exactly," Fiona said.

"Do you know if there are others in town who are looking?" Clint asked.

"Not for sure," she said, "but why else would somebody shoot the poor little guy?"

"Little guy?" Artie asked.

"He was little, wasn't he?" she asked.

"But weren't you and him—I mean," Artie stammered, "you and him were, uh—"

"Oh, Jesus, no!" Fiona said. "We were supposed to be partners."

"Really?" Clint asked. "I thought Artie and Eddie were partners."

"And you?" she asked. "What do you bring to the party? Besides the obvious, I mean."

"The obvious?" Clint asked. "Oh, you mean my gun. No, I'm not hiring out my gun."

"But if you're a partner, your gun is part of you, right?" she asked.

"My gun is always part of me," he said.

"Clint's in it for the backin'," Artie said. "I don't have any money."

"And neither did Eddie," Fiona said. "So that's where I came in."

"So then you know whether or not he got a boat," Clint said.

"Yes," she said, "he got a boat, with my money."

"So we're good," Artie said. "We've got the boat."

"Yeah," Clint said, "but wasn't Eddie going to point out where the gold is?"

"He was," Artie said, "but he told me a lot of things."

"You think you can find the gold?" Clint asked.

"I think I wanna try." Artie looked at Fiona. "What about you?"

"He did a lot of talkin' to me, too," she said. "Maybe between us we can find it."

"So you're in?" Artie asked.

"I'm in," she said.

"What about you, Clint?"

"I'm in," Clint said. "I don't like what happened to Eddie." He looked at Fiona. "I'll give you half what the boat cost."

"Suits me," she said. "You fellas wanna see it?"

"Sure," Artie said.

"Let's go down to the docks, then."

***

They stood on the dock looking at the boat Eddie Lee had purchased.

"What is it?" Artie asked.

"It's called a flatboat," Fiona said.

Clint studied it. It was about 40 feet long, with no cabin for shelter.

"What do we do if it rains?"

"Get to shore," Fiona said, "or take cover under a tarp."

"How is it powered?" Artie asked.

"Shoulder poles," she said, "and oars. Anything bigger would take more than the three of us."

Artie frowned.

"It don't look big enough for me, let alone what we're gonna be transporting."

"Don't worry," she said. "Eddie said we could make as many trips as we have to in that boat. In fact, he said that with what we bring back the first time, we can hire a bigger one, and maybe even a crew. But he said a flatboat can hold a lot of weight."

"We don't want a crew wondering what we're taking off the shore," Clint said. "Do we?"

"Not a chance," Artie said. "Once we locate the . . ." he lowered his voice, ". . . stuff, we can come back with a wagon big enough to transport it all. We only need the boat to find it."

Artie had told Clint that once before. This was for Fiona's benefit.

"Then we're all set," Clint said, "except for wondering who shot Eddie Lee."

"And not gettin' shot ourselves," Artie said.

"Isn't that where it comes in handy havin' the Gunsmith as a partner?" Fiona asked.

Clint didn't say anything, so after a moment Artie said, "Yeah, I guess it is."

Chapter Ten

They decided to have supper together, spend some time getting to know each other a little more.

"How did you and Eddie meet?" Clint asked.

"I heard him in a saloon, asking about a boat," she said. "From the kind he was looking for, I figured out he needed to transport some cargo. So I asked him."

"And he told you?"

"He did," she said. "He was real talkative. I think he thought he was gonna get into my room. But in the end, we agreed all he'd get from me was money."

"How much talking did Eddie do around town?" Clint asked. "I mean, before he met you?"

"I don't know," she said. "Probably quite a bit. Oh, you're thinkin' that's why he was shot? He talked too much?"

"Could be."

"Eddie did have a big mouth," Artie said. "He told me the first mate was always tellin' him to shut up."

"Looks like he finally spoke once too many times," Clint said.

"Okay, I don't want to be mean," Fiona said, "but he was your friend, not mine."

"Not mine" Clint said. "I never knew him. He was Artie's friend."

"Not a friend so much as a partner," Artie said. "I mean, I didn't know him that well."

"Then why partner with him?" Clint asked.

"Because he actually served on the Far West," Artie said. "If anyone could find that gold, it would've been him."

"But he told me things," Fiona said, "and he told you things. So we could stay here and mourn him, or just get on with it. We've got the boat."

"That's another thing," Clint said. "He was the one who knew boats. I've been on paddleboats and steamships, but I don't know the first thing about smaller boats. Aren't we going to need somebody to operate the thing?"

"That would mean splitting with someone else," Fiona said, "and right now I like the idea of a three-way split."

Clint wondered if she so liked the idea of a three-way split that she would've had Eddie Lee killed?

"What did Eddie get us?" Clint asked Fiona.

"A flatboat."

"I've been on flatboats before," Artie said.

"So have I," Fiona said.

"You both have enough experience for this?" Clint asked, wondering if one or both of them were lying?

The Treasure of Little Bighorn

"We can get it done," Artie said. "You need at least three people to navigate it, depending on the size. We'll have to see."

"I agree," Fiona said.

"All right, then," Clint said. "We'll need supplies."

"I laid out the money for the boat, remember," Fiona said.

"I'll get the supplies," Clint said, "and then reimburse you for my half of the boat."

"We'll have to buy everythin' tomorrow," she said.

"So then we can leave the day after," Artie said. "That'll give me time to look the boat over, get familiar with it."

"I'll need to do that, too," Fiona said.

"We can go back there and do that now," Artie suggested. "Also, make sure it's properly tied off and safe."

"You two do that," Clint said.

"What are you gonna do?" Fiona asked.

"I want to talk to the sheriff again," he said.

"About what?" Artie asked.

"I want to see what he's got on Eddie Lee's shooting," Clint said. "I want to try to figure out if we're going to have further trouble like that."

"I would say yes," Fiona said. "After all, treasure hunting is dangerous business."

"So you've done this before?" Clint asked. "Gone treasure hunting?"

"I have," she said, "and there's always somebody on your tail, or tryin' to get there ahead of you."

When the waiter brought the check, Clint grabbed it.

"Time for me to start paying you back," he said to Fiona.

"I can think of some other ways, too," she purred.

Artie seemed to miss the implication, but Clint didn't.

Chapter Eleven

When Clint walked into the sheriff's office the man looked up from some paperwork he was doing.

"Mr. Adams." he said, putting his pencil down. "Did you get your friend taken care of?"

"He wasn't my friend," Clint said, "but yes, he's taken care of."

"Good, good. So what can I do for you?"

"Do you know why Eddie Lee was here in town?" Clint asked.

"Actually, no I don't," the sheriff said. "His woman wouldn't tell me."

"She wasn't his woman," Clint said, "just his partner."

"Yeah, she told me that," Dayton admitted, "but partners in what? That she wouldn't tell me."

"They're both hunters," Clint told him.

"Bounty hunters?"

"Treasure hunters."

"Ah," Dayton said. "You know, living near the river you run into all kinds of treasure hunters. What are these two lookin' for?"

"I can't say, exactly," Clint said, "but it's a possibility that's why he was shot the way he was."

"You mean other hunters?" Dayton asked.

Clint nodded.

"Do you know of any others in town?" Clint asked. "I mean, you may not know what they're hunting for, but you might have seen them, or heard about them."

Dayton sat back in his chair.

"No, I can't say that I have." He looked at Clint. "You wouldn't be plannin' on findin' them and takin' some kind of revenge, would you? I don't need that kind of thing in my town."

"No," Clint said, "that's not my plan, at all. In fact, we'll be leaving day after tomorrow. But if anyone tries anything before then . . ."

"You'll protect yourself," Dayton said. "I get that."

"Good," Clint said. "But I'd be very happy never to take my gun out of my holster while I'm here."

"Well," Sheriff Dayton said, "I'm glad to hear that. You gonna be in the Paddleboat?"

"Yep," Clint said, "like I said, til day after tomorrow."

"If I come up with any information I think will be helpful, I'll let you know."

"I'd appreciate that," Clint said. He looked around. "You got any deputies?"

"Don't need one," Dayton said. "This is just a little river town. Nothing ever happens."

"Until Eddie Lee got shot."

"Well, yeah," the lawman said, "there is that. But I'm still lookin' into it."

"Good luck," Clint said, and left, not feeling very confident that Sheriff Dayton would find who killed Eddie Lee.

***

"She's a tough one," Artie Small said.

He and Clint were standing at the bar in the Paddleboat Saloon, actually waiting for Fiona to come down from her room. After she and Artie had returned from the dock she said she wanted to change before they went to supper.

"How so?" Clint asked.

"We examined the boat, and at one point she was bending over to have a look at the stern."

"And you were looking at her stern?"

"Yeah."

"And she caught you?"

"Yeah, and she almost knocked me off the boat. She's strong!"

"She hit you?"

"She shoved me," Artie said, "and I ain't easy to shove."

"I guess we're going to have to watch out step."

"But she's a good-lookin' woman."

"Yeah, she is."

"And we're gonna be on that little boat with her for a while."

"What is it, forty feet?"

"Yeah," Artie said. "We measured it. And twelve feet wide."

"Well, Artie," Clint said, "that means that at any time you can be forty feet away from her."

"That's probably what she wants," Artie said, sullenly.

"So let's give the lady what she wants and then we can all get what we want."

"Yeah, I guess."

They sat at their same table, because the saloon still wasn't full. Off the beaten path, Clint was pretty sure it was always like this, which suited him.

They were both drinking their beers when Fiona came through the batwing doors from outside. They each stopped and put their mugs down. Fiona had changed from her man's shirt and jeans into a dress that hugged her and showed her shoulders and arms.

"Jesus," Artie Small said. "Forty feet may not be enough."

Chapter Twelve

Fiona walked over to them, followed by the eyes of the others in the saloon, as few as there were.

"Hey, boys," she said, sitting with them. "Hungry?"

Her auburn hair was hanging down past her shoulders and looked as if it had recently been washed.

"You look great," Clint said.

"Thank you," she said. "I thought I'd take the opportunity to dress like a lady before we get on the river. There I'll just be another river rat."

"You ain't never gonna look like no river rat," Artie told her.

"Thank you, Artie," she said, "but please don't think this means you can grab my butt again."

"He grabbed you?" Clint asked.

"On the boat," she said. "He grabbed me, and I slapped him."

"I thought she was fallin'," Artie argued.

"You didn't tell me she slapped you."

Artie felt his face.

"It was embarrassin'," he explained. "And hard."

"Do you want a drink before we eat?" Clint asked her.

"No, why don't we just go."

"Do you know a good place?" Clint asked. "We just got to town, so . . ."

"I know a place," she said, standing. "Come on."

"Are we under dressed?" Clint asked, as they walked to the door.

"Don't worry," she said. "I dressed this way just for me. It won't matter."

***

It didn't.

She took them to a busy steakhouse that had customers who were dressed in all different attire.

"See?" she said, as they entered. "No problem."

"This place is too crowded," Clint said.

"You don't like crowds?"

"Not when so many of them have guns."

"Don't worry," she said. "There are private rooms in the back."

Private rooms? Clint wondered how she had found this place?

When a 50ish man in a tuxedo came to greet them, he smiled at Fiona.

"You're back," he said. "How nice. Private room?"

"Please," Fiona said.

He ushered them across the crowded floor to a curtained doorway, which led to a room with one table.

"Champagne?" he asked.

"I think three beers would be fine," Clint said.

The man looked at Fiona, who said, "That's fine."

"Your waiter will be right here," the man said.

"How did you find this place?" Clint finally asked.

"I got to town even before Eddie," she said. "I was lookin' for a place to eat, and somebody told me about this one."

"They gave you a private room just for you?" Artie asked.

She smiled. "What makes you think I was alone?"

Clint laughed at the look on Artie's face. The big man was smitten. When he stopped laughing he hoped it wouldn't become a problem.

A waiter entered carrying three beers, and Fiona ordered steak dinners for all of them. When the food came, they started eating, and didn't do any talking except for Fiona saying, "I'm starvin'."

Artie remained silent, alone with his own thoughts, but he kept looking at Fiona. Clint thought he knew what those thoughts were.

"Dessert?" the waiter asked.

"Coffee and three of those delicious apple pies," Fiona said. She looked at Clint and Artie. "Okay?"

"Sure," Clint said, even though he preferred peach.

Artie just nodded.

"How was that?" Fiona asked. "As good as I said it would be?"

"Yes," Clint said, "very good."

"And you?" she asked, looking at Artie.

He nodded his head and said, "Good."

"Wait til you taste the pie."

But before the pies arrived Artie stood up and said, "I gotta go."

"But the pie—" Fiona started.

"I gotta walk," he said. "I'll see you back at the Paddleboat."

As he went through the curtains Clint called out, "Watch your back!"

"What's wrong with him?" she asked.

"You don't know?"

"Is he mad because I slapped him?"

"I don't think mad is the word," Clint said.

"Embarrassed?"

"Not that, either."

"Okay, I give up," she said, shaking her head. "What's the word?"

He looked at her and said, "Love."

Chapter Thirteen

"What?"

"He's in love with you," Clint said.

"I thought he was just gettin' grabby this afternoon," she said.

"Artie doesn't really do that," Clint said. "Unless he's changed a lot since I last saw him. No, I think you're going to have him following you around like a puppy for a while."

She frowned. "I thought I was going to have that problem with Eddie Lee."

"And then somebody killed him."

She looked at Clint. "You think there was a connection? And that somebody's going to try to kill Artie because of me?"

"Because of you, or the treasure," Clint said. "Is there somebody else in town who's a conquest of yours?"

"I haven't been here long enough for that."

"I beg to differ," he said. "Already you've conquered Eddie Lee and Artie."

"Well, I assure you there's nobody else," she said, then added, "unless you . . ."

"Sorry," Clint said. "Right now I'm more interested in keeping Artie alive and finding the treasure."

"Fine," she said, "that's what I'm interested in, too."

"Good," Clint said, "then we're thinking alike."

***

They finished their pie and coffee and started walking back to the hotel. When they turned onto Rust Street Fiona started getting looks.

"They haven't seen anything like you around here," Clint told her.

"And they won't see me again in a couple of days, when we get on the river," she said.

"That's true."

"And we won't see much more than the river and the shore for a while."

"That's true, too."

"So I'm glad we had this supper out," she said.

"So am I."

When they reached the hotel they entered the lobby, looking around for Artie.

"I hope he's in his room," she said, as they went up the steps.

"I'll check on him," Clint said.

He walked her to her door and waited while she unlocked it.

She leaned in and kissed him on the cheek. Her scent lingered in his nostrils.

"Thanks for bein' a gentleman and walkin' me to my door," she said.

"Good-night," he said.

"See you for breakfast?" she asked. "Then we can pick up our supplies."

"Good. See you then."

She went inside and closed her door. He waited to hear the lock, then walked to Artie's door and knocked.

"Come on in," Artie said, morosely.

Clint entered, saw half a bottle of whiskey on the table next to the bed.

"Artie," he said, "there's not going to be any whiskey on the boat."

"I know," Artie said, sitting on the bed. "That's why I got it now."

"Also," Clint said, "we need to talk about Fiona."

"What about her?"

"Don't fall in love with her."

"Too late," he said.

"No," Clint said, "it isn't. Fall out of love with her."

"Just like that?" He looked even more miserable at the prospect.

"Yeah, just like that," Clint said. "Think about why we're here, Artie."

"Custer's gold."

"*The* gold," Clint said. "Custer had nothing to do with it. But yes, gold."

Artie grabbed the whiskey bottle, and Clint quickly snatched it from his hand.

"Gold, Artie," he said, again. "Just keep thinking about gold. Okay?"

"Yeah, okay."

"I'll come and get you for breakfast," Clint said.

"You, me and Fiona?"

"That's right."

Artie took a deep breath.

"Yeah," he said, finally, "okay, let's have breakfast."

"Good-night, Artie."

Clint headed for the door, with the bottle.

***

In his room he set the bottle aside and sat on the bed. He hoped that the way Artie felt about Fiona was not going to be a problem.

Chapter Fourteen

Clint decided to get a drink.

He didn't want the whiskey he had taken from Artie, so he left the bottle on the chest of drawers, next to the pitcher-and-basin, and left his room. He figured to just go next door to the Paddleboat Saloon and have a beer. Maybe after that he would be ready to go to sleep and start the next day as a treasure hunter.

As he went by the desk clerk the man looked away, leading Clint to believe he had something to tell him.

"What's going on?" he asked, stopping at the desk.

"Huh? Oh, nothin'—"

"Yeah, something is. What is it?"

"Um, she told me not to say anythin'."

"Who did?"

"The woman," he said, "from room one."

"Fiona?"

"Um, yeah."

"Where'd she go?"

"Uh, a few streets from here there's a saloon," the clerk said.

"What's it called?"

"The Long Dive Saloon."

"Long Dive?"

The clerk nodded.

"It's, uh, a few steps below the Paddleboat."

"So, it's pretty bad."

"Yeah," the man said. "I think they call it that because it's a pretty long dive, uh, down."

"And do you know why she went there?"

"No," the clerk said. "But I think . . ."

"Think what? Come on, say it."

"I think she was lookin' for, you know, a man."

"A certain man?"

"No," he said, "just a man, uh, you know, for the night."

"What makes you think that?"

"Because of the way she was dressed."

"And?"

"And I've seen lots of women come in here with men," the clerk said, "and she had that look in her eye."

"Okay," Clint said, "how do I get to the Long Dive?"

***

On one hand Clint should have just let Fiona do whatever she wanted to do. She was, after all, a grown woman, and a capable one. But he couldn't afford to have her get herself killed, the way Eddie Lee did. So he was determined to find her and bring her back before she got into trouble.

When he got to the Long Dive Saloon he saw what the hotel clerk meant. As low class as the Paddleboat looked, this place made that one seem classy. The windows were so dirty he couldn't see inside. One of the batwing doors was hanging by one hinge. The base of the building looked charred, as if it had once been on fire.

He went to the doors and looked over them to the inside. He saw Fiona right away, standing at the bar, still wearing the same dress. All of the men in the place were staring at her. She was holding a glass of whiskey.

Clint entered and walked right to the bar.

"Do you have a death wish?" he asked.

She turned her head and looked at him.

"What are you doin' here?"

"Trying to keep you from making a big mistake."

"What kind of mistake do you think I'm makin'?" she asked.

"You're going to get yourself killed."

"I'm here for exactly the opposite reason," she told him.

"What reason."

She leaned into him.

"I'm lookin' to get fucked."

"Why tonight?"

"Because who knows when the next time will be?" she asked. "I just need it tonight, Clint. With no . . . connections. No attachments."

"If that's the case," he said, trying not to look shocked, "I'm sure Artie would have been happy to help you."

"No, no," she said, "not Artie. Not somebody I'm gonna be seeing every day for . . . who knows how long." She sounded like she'd had a few whiskeys before he got there. "Besides, do you really think Artie could fuck me and not have any attachments, after?"

"No, you're right about that. So then who?" Clint asked. "One of these men?"

"What's wrong with these men?" she asked.

Clint looked around.

"They're dregs," he said.

"All the more reason why I'd never see him again."

"Obviously."

"I have it narrowed down to two," she said. "But I'm waiting to see if one of them will step up."

Clint looked around, again. He was getting dirty looks from more than one man who was probably considering it.

"No, no," he said, "not tonight. Come on."

"Where?"

"Back to the hotel," Clint said. "We have a lot to do starting tomorrow."

She stared at him, then said, "All right. I'll go back with you."

She put her glass down and they walked to the front doors. There she turned and said, wistfully, "Sorry, boys."

***

They walked back to the hotel in silence, with Fiona still drawing looks from men they passed on the street. She was, after all, a statuesque six feet tall, with the kind of body men dreamed about, and would die for.

When they reached the hotel they walked through the lobby, the clerk was pretending to have a lot of work on his desk and was not looking at them.

"He did his best not to tell me where you went," Clint told her.

"That's okay."

"What about him?" Clint asked. "Did you consider him?"

She looked over at the clerk.

"No, no, not for a second."

"Why not?"

She smiled.

"I'd break him in half," she said, laughing, "don't you think?"

Clint looked over at the man.

"Yeah, I guess you would."

They went up the steps and stopped in front of room one.

"Okay," he said, "so we have this sorted out?"

"We do," she said, unlocking her door.

"So I'll see you in the morning."

"Yes," she said, turning to face him, her back to the room, "you will—and all you'll have to do is roll over."

"What?"

She reached out and grabbed the front of his shirt in both hands.

"And thank you for volunteering."

She started to tug him into the room but he dug in his heels.

"Whoa, wait," he said. "When did I volunteer?"

"At the saloon," she said. "You volunteered, and I accept you."

"Wait, Fiona—"

She released his shirt, stepped back, reached behind her and shrugged her dress to the floor.

Standing before him, totally and gloriously naked, she asked, "Is there a problem?"

Chapter Fifteen

Once he was in the room there was no turning back. They just had to make sure Artie Small never found out.

Clint closed the door behind him and stared at Fiona.

"Well?" she asked.

"You're beautiful," he said.

"I didn't bring you in here to talk, Clint," she said. "Let's get this done so you can go back to your own room, and we both can get some sleep."

He closed the distance between them, reached to pull her close and kiss her. She swatted his hands away.

"No kissing," she said. "Just fucking. And for that you have to get your clothes off."

"Oh, right," he said, and proceeded to disrobe, first hanging his gun belt on her bedpost.

"You usually keep that close?" she asked.

"No," he said, "not usually—always."

She pulled down the sheet and reclined on the bed, watching him undress.

"Now, don't forget," she told him. "No attachments, so there's no complications."

"Right."

"You know what I'm after," she said. "A hard, fast fuck."

Her attitude was starting to annoy him, so he said, "Oh, that's what you're going to get, don't worry."

"You know, Artie would've been good for this," she said. "He's more my type than you are."

"Is that right?"

"Yeah, I usually pick big men."

"I'll try to make up for my lack of size in other ways," he said.

He watched her face as he took off his underwear and his semi-erect cock sprang into view. It wasn't fully erect because she wasn't supplying a sexy attitude. True, she was naked, and her breasts were imposing, topped with large, dark nipples, and the pubic thatch between her large thighs was busy. But other than that, she wasn't giving off any kind of signals.

"Now, be careful," she said, as he climbed onto the bed with her, "I'm not exactly wet . . ."

"We can fix that," he said, sliding his hand down over her pubic hair, stroking her with his fingertips.

"Oh," she said, "what're you—oh!"

Suddenly she was wet, and he was stroking her clit while inserting his thumb into her vagina.

"Oh, God," she said, "where did you learn—ooh."

"Is that wet enough?" he asked.

"Well, no," she said, "I could be, uh, wetter . . ."

"Okay," he said, "since you asked . . ."

He slid down between her legs, pressed his face to her and replaced his fingers with his lips and tongue. Fiona was easily a woman in her 30s, but apparently a man had never taken the time to do this for her, before.

She wrapped her incredibly strong, long legs around him, reached down to hold his head while he continued to excite her with his mouth.

"Jesus," she gasped, bucking, lifting her butt up to meet the pressure of his mouth, "Oh God . . ."

When her time came she released his head and beat her fists on the bed, riding out the sensations he had sent through her with his mouth.

Raising himself above her he said, "I think you're wet enough now. What do you think?"

"Fuck me, you bastard!" she snapped, her eyes flashing.

He pushed her legs apart, knelt between them and drove his hard penis into her soaking vagina.

"Oooh, God!" she gasped, and once again he felt those powerful legs wrap around him.

He started to pound into her as brutally as he could. She was a large, solid woman who was able to not only take it but give back in kind. Before long they had the bed leaping off the floor, sounding like it might fall apart. They both filled the room with their grunts. Finally, he exploded inside of her with a great roar, which she followed with a muffled scream. When he rolled off of her onto his back, he suddenly hoped that Artie, just down the hall, hadn't heard them.

"Omigod!" she said, covering her face with her hands.

"I know," he said.

"That was . . . that was . . ." she gasped.

"I know," he said, again. "For me, too. But remember what you said. No attachments."

"Right."

"We can't let this affect our time together on the boat."

"No, we can't."

"And we can't let Artie find out," Clint said.

"Definitely not," she agreed.

He sat up, swung his feet to the floor.

"Well, now that I've given you what you wanted—"

"—you sure have."

"—I better get to my own room. We're going to need some sleep."

"Yeah, we are," she said, reaching for him and grabbing his arm to stop him from rising.

"What?" he asked.

She got to her knees behind him, pressed her breasts to his back, and reached around to grasp his cock.

"Let's go again just to be sure we got it right!"

Chapter Sixteen

Clint woke in the morning with Fiona down between his legs, his hard cock in her mouth as she avidly sucked him. It was a nice way to wake up, and had happened to him before, but this time he reacted differently.

"Fiona, Jesus—" he said, trying to pry her mouth off of him. "What the hell happened? Did I fall asleep?"

They'd had sex again, and if he had fallen asleep that soundly, he was livid with himself. For one thing, anybody could have killed him in his sleep. And secondly, what if Artie had gone to his room looking for him.

"Let me finish you—" she complained, but he struggled to get away from her and to his feet.

"I have to get back to my own room," he said, "hopefully without Artie seeing me."

She rolled over and leaned her head on her hand, looking up at him.

"Are you going to run down the hall with that wagging ahead of you?"

He looked down at his rigid penis, and hurriedly pulled his trousers on over it.

"Remember," he said, "not a word to Artie."

"Not a peep."

"We'll come and get you for breakfast."

"I'll be ready. Oh, and Clint."

He stopped at the door and turned back.

"Thank you," she said. "And remember, no attachments."

He left.

***

In his own room he sat on the bed and shook his head. What a mistake last night had been. The events could have blown up in all their faces. Sex with Fiona had been more than pleasant, but certainly not worth losing $375,000 in gold . . . or his life.

He hurriedly washed himself using the pitcher-and-basin in the room, and then got dressed, just as the knock came on the door.

"I thought we were goin' to breakfast," Artie Small complained. "I'm starved."

"I was just coming to get you," Clint said.

"Well, let's see if Fiona's ready. After all, she's a woman and we're probably gonna have to wait for her."

"We might be surprised," Clint said.

Artie was surprised, because when Fiona opened her door. She was bright-eyed, alert and happy. She was dressed once again for work, in shirt, jeans and boots, and her hair was pulled back behind her head.

"It's about time!" she said. "I'm hungry."

"So am I," Artie said. "Let's get a move on."

"Good-morning," Clint said, as Artie rushed ahead of them.

"Good-morning."

"Sleep well?" he asked.

"Like a baby," she said, smiling.

They walked through the lobby, stepped outside and found Artie looking in all directions.

"Where to?" he asked. "I'm ready for some steak-and-eggs."

"Then follow me," Fiona said. "Somebody told me about a place."

"Who?" Artie asked.

"Just somebody I met here in town before you fellas showed up."

Artie frowned. He was obviously thinking it was somebody she'd slept with.

"Lead the way, then," Clint said. "Steak-and-eggs always sounds good to me."

She walked them a few blocks to a small café that looked like it was doing a brisk breakfast business. It also seemed fairly new; the building didn't look as if it was going to fall down any minute.

"Why didn't we come here before?" Artie asked.

"I was told they're only open for breakfast."

Once inside they saw that most of the tables were occupied. Clint wanted one against the wall, but they were told they'd have to wait for that. There was one near the front window, and Fiona offered to sit with her back to the glass, so that Clint could sit opposite her, with a clear view out. Since he had already done something stupid the night before that could have gotten him killed, he agreed.

When a waiter came over they all ordered steak-and-eggs and coffee.

"So, what's on the agenda today?" Clint asked, when they were all eating.

"Get the boat ready to go," Fiona said. "Artie can start making it shipshape while you and me go and get some supplies."

"I gotta work on the boat alone?" Artie complained.

"Until we get there," Fiona said. "Then we'll load the supplies on board and help you."

"Can we leave tonight?" Artie asked.

"If you want to be on the river after dark, sure," she said. "But without Eddie Lee, we might run into something, or run aground. We better wait until morning."

"That sounds like a plan," Clint said.

"Yeah, okay," Artie agreed, morosely.

"Come on, Artie," Fiona said, lowering her voice and putting her hand and on his shoulder, "buck up. We're going to be rich."

"Yeah, we are," he said, giving her the ghost of a smile.

From that point on they ate and didn't talk.

***

After breakfast Clint and Fiona walked Artie down to the dock, where the boat was still waiting.

"What do I do?" he asked.

"Have you ever been on a boat before?" Fiona asked.

"Well, yeah . . ."

"A riverboat, right?" Clint asked.

Artie nodded. "A paddlewheeler."

"Well," Fiona said, "I've used poles and oars, so I guess I'm a little ahead of you fellas."

"Just make sure the boat is sound, Artie," Clint said. He slapped his friend on the back. "If it holds you, it'll hold anybody."

Artie smiled.

"You got that right!" he said.

"We'll be back soon."

As they started to walk away Fiona asked Clint, "You want to go back to my bed?"

"Stop that!" he scolded her. "No attachments, remember?"

"I'm not attached," she told him. "I just want to fuck some more."

In spite of himself Clint said, "Well . . . maybe to-night."

Chapter Seventeen

They went to the mercantile nearest to the dock for their supplies.

"Food and rope is mostly what we need," Fiona said, as they entered. "Maybe some tools."

"What about poles and oars?" Clint asked.

"They're on the boat."

"Do we need extras?"

"Poles maybe," Fiona admitted, after a moment. "They've been known to snap."

They moved around the store, finding what they needed, picking up what they could carry themselves, and asking the clerk for other things, plus the poles and oars.

"You gonna be on the river?" the clerk asked.

"We are," Fiona said.

"You got leadlines?"

"Damn!" Fiona said. "I didn't think of that."

"Don't matter what size boat you're on, you're gonna have to check the river depth. You'll need a leadline for that."

"Okay, then," Clint said. "Add that to our purchases."

"I don't think we need a leadline with a flat-bottomed boat," Fiona said.

"Better safe than sorry," Clint said.

She shrugged. "You're laying out the funds for this shopping spree."

"Right."

In addition to everything else, they bought cartridges for Clint's guns, and Artie's Henry rifle, and an extra Winchester rifle for Fiona.

"I thought you were going to do all the shooting?" she said.

"You never know," Clint told her.

They arranged to pick up all the supplies early the next morning, with a rented buckboard.

"Why not tonight?" Fiona asked, as they left the store.

"We don't want to load the boat up and have it all stolen overnight," Clint said.

"Good point," she said. "What next?"

"I'd like to stop in on the sheriff and see if he's found out anything about who killed Eddie Lee."

"Suits me," she said. "I'll come along."

"Sure you don't want to go to the dock and help Artie?" he asked.

"I'm positive."

***

Dayton looked up smiled when he saw Fiona. He only seemed to notice Clint a few moments later.

"Adams," he said, "what can I do for you and the lady?"

"Sheriff," Clint said, "you do know—" Clint realized at that point that he had never heard Fiona's last name, "—the lady."

"I questioned Miss Shay after her friend, Ed Lee, was killed."

"Not my friend, Sheriff," she said, "my partner. I told you that."

"Right, right. Well, what can I do for the two of you?"

"We were just wondering if you'd made any progress on Eddie Lee's shooting."

"Afraid I haven't," the lawman said. "He didn't know many people in town."

"Were you going on the assumption he was killed by somebody he knew?"

"That was how I started," the sheriff said. "I'm afraid I'm gonna have to change my tactic, though."

"I see," Clint said.

"Is there anything else either of you can tell me?" Dayton asked.

"Afraid not," Clint said. "We're just as much in the dark as you are."

"And when will you be leaving town?" Dayton asked.

"In the morning."

"On a boat, right?"

"That's right."

"So you'll be leaving your horses in town?"

"I don't have a horse," Fiona said, but the sheriff's question reminded Clint that he had Eclipse with him. What was he going to do to keep the Darley Arabian safe?

"I put mine in your town livery," Clint said. "What do you know about the hostler there?"

"That's Willie Jackson. If you value your horse, I wouldn't depend on him to care for it. On the other hand, Lew Bishop has a barn at the north end of town. He's a good horseman. With an animal like yours, you need somebody like Lew."

"Thanks, Sheriff," Clint said. "I'll check that out."

"And I guess," Dayton said, "I'll see you when you come back to get him."

"Yes, you will," Clint said. "Hopefully, you'll know something by then about Lee's killer."

"Depend on it," the man said. "Murder in my town? I'm not about to let that go."

"That's good to hear," Clint said. "Thanks."

"Ma'am," Dayton said. "Have a safe trip."

"Thank you, Sheriff," Fiona said.

They left the office. Just outside the door Clint looked at Fiona.

"Shay? Doesn't really go with Fiona, does it?" he asked.

"It was my husband's last name."

"You're married?"

"Was," she said. "It's a long story. Should we see about your horse?"

"Yes," Clint said, "that's next."

Chapter Eighteen

Clint didn't waste any time. He took Eclipse out of the town livery and walked him—along with Fiona—to the north end of town, where they saw the barn the sheriff had mentioned. It looked well built, and clean, both of which were encouraging. The two large front doors were closed.

Clint walked to the doors and banged on them with the flat of his left hand.

"You do everything with your left hand?" she asked. "To protect the right?"

"I shoot with the right hand," he said. "I don't do everything else left handed, but I do protect my right. The day I can't pulled the trigger will probably be the day I die."

"That's not an easy way to live, is it?"

"Not easy," he said, "but you get used to it."

He banged on the doors again. This time he heard them being unlocked, and then one swung open. A bandy-legged man about 5 ½ feet tall stared out at him.

"Can't you see my doors are closed and locked?"

"Are you Lew Bishop?"

"I am."

"The sheriff suggested I bring my horse to you," Clint said.

"Why?"

"I'm leaving town on a boat, and I have to keep him here for a while," Clint said. "I can't trust him to just anybody."

"Him?"

"That's right."

"Where is he?"

"Right there." Clint pointed.

The man stuck his head out for a look and raised his eyebrows when he was Eclipse.

"Jesus," he said, coming out. "What a beauty."

He approached Eclipse, still hadn't seen Fiona standing on the other side of Clint. He examined the Darley, running his hands over his neck, withers, and his legs.

"He's not young, but he's in great condition,"

"Yes, he is."

"How long do you want to leave him with me?"

"I'm not sure how long I'll be gone," Clint admitted.

"That's fine," Bishop said. "I'll take him. Do you know why?"

"Because he's a beauty?"

"That," Bishop said, "and because you referred to him as 'him.' I hate people who refer to horses as things."

Bishop took Eclipse's reins, turned to walk him into the barn, and then saw Fiona.

"Jesus," he said, "what a beauty."

Chapter Nineteen

With Eclipse taken care of—Clint appreciated Bishop's attitude and respect for the Darley Arabian—Clint and Fiona's next step was to rent a buckboard. In fact, he asked Bishop if he knew where to get one.

"For how long?" the man asked.

"Just tomorrow morning, to take some supplies to the dock," Clint said. "We'd bring it right back."

"You got it," Bishop said. "You can pick it up in the morning."

"Thanks."

As they walked away from Lew Bishop's barn Fiona said, "So what about now?"

"For what?"

"You know, more fucking."

Clint stopped walking, turned to face her.

"Fiona, you're not going to be able to do this on the boat," he said.

"We're not on the boat, yet," she told him. "I'm just looking to go one more time before we leave."

"We'll see about tonight."

"Come on," she said, "you liked it as much as I did."

"Liked it?" he asked. "I loved it. That's beside the point."

"Yes, I know," Fiona said, "poor Artie, he's in love with me."

"We've got to make sure we all keep our minds on business," Clint said, "and our business is finding that gold."

"Okay, fine," she said, "so what now?"

"Let's go to the dock and see what Artie's doing," Clint said. "If he's done he's going to be hungry."

"Is he always hungry?"

"Pretty much. We're going to use food to distract him from you."

"If that works," she said, "it's not going to be very flattering."

***

When they reached the boat, Artie was sitting on the dock with his legs dangling, staring out at the river.

"Finished?" Clint asked.

"There ain't much to this boat," the big man said. "I wonder if Eddie made a good buy."

"Is it solid?" Clint asked.

"Solid enough, I guess," Artie said. "The question is, is it big enough."

"It looks big enough for the three of us," Fiona commented.

"I know," Artie said, getting to his feet. "Now! What about," he lowered his voice, "you know, when we have . . . cargo?"

"We're not going to have that much, Artie," Clint said. "For one thing, we won't be able to lift it. We're just going to locate it so we can go back later by wagon and get it. We'll just bring a few bars back with us, you know, for expenses."

Fiona also lowered her voice.

"A bar each is going to go a long way."

"Probably," Clint said, "but we're also going to have to look for somebody to take it off our hands for a fair price."

Fiona looked at Artie.

"I thought since you and Eddie started, that you had somebody."

"Eddie had somebody in mind," Artie said.

"Who?" Clint asked.

"I don't know," Artie said. "He didn't tell me."

"He didn't tell you?" Fiona asked. "You mean, he didn't trust you?"

"Eddie didn't trust anybody."

"Might be one of the reasons he got shot," Clint said.

"Does the sheriff know anythin', yet?" Artie asked.

"No, not yet," Clint said. "But he seemed determined. He doesn't like the idea of a murder happening in his town."

"Can we get some lunch now?" Artie asked.

Clint looked at the sky.

"It's early," he said. "I've got an idea."

"What?" Artie asked.

"Just in case somebody's watching us, getting ready to do what they did to Eddie," Clint said, "let's leave now."

"What?" Artie said.

"Right now?" Fiona asked.

"That's my suggestion," Clint said. "We know where to get a buckboard. We can go get the supplies, load them on the boat, make it look like we're loading to leave tomorrow."

"We did say that to the man at the mercantile, and to Lew Bishop," Fiona said.

"Who's Lew Bishop?" Artie asked.

"He's taking care of my horse while we're away, and loaning us a buckboard. We told him we needed it in the morning, but we can go and get it now."

"So if they're watchin' us load," Artie said, "and they think we're gonna leave in the mornin'—"

"We jump on the boat and leave as soon as we get loaded," Clint finished.

"I like it," Fiona said.

"What about eatin'?"

Clint put his hand on Artie's big shoulder.

"We'll do that, too."

"Then I'm in!"

Chapter Twenty

Bishop had no problem giving them the buckboard a day early.

"Leave it on the dock if you like," he told them. "I'll pick it up."

"We can bring it back," Clint said.

"I get the feelin' you changed your minds about leavin' tomorrow for a reason," he said. "If the buckboard is on the dock, it'll look like you're not leavin'."

"Good point," Fiona said.

"Thanks, Beauty," Bishop said, with a smile.

"Hey—" Artie started.

"Relax, Artie," Fiona said, "the man's just being nice."

"Yeah, take it easy, big fella," Bishop said.

"It's okay," Clint said, grabbing Artie's arm, "he's just hungry. Let's get him a sandwich."

They all got on the buckboard and, thanking Bishop once again, drove it away.

***

While Clint and Fiona loaded the supplies onto the buckboard, Artie went across the street for a sandwich. He came back with three, munching on his already.

"We'll eat ours once we get going," Clint said. "Let's go to the dock."

Bishop had given them one horse to pull the buckboard, which was enough. He seemed fairly certain that no one was going to steal either when Clint and company left them behind.

"Folks in town know me," Bishop said.

"That's good," Clint said.

When they got to the dock the three of them unloaded their supplies onto the boat, Artie working with his sandwich in one hand and, occasionally, sticking out of his mouth. Once the supplies were stowed, they covered them with a tarp.

"Okay," Clint said, "let's get on. Artie, as soon as we do, you untie us and shove off from the dock."

"Right."

"Fiona, you and me, we'll get on the poles. In minutes we'll be too far from the dock for anybody to try anything."

"Except maybe shoot," Artie said.

"Let's see what happens."

They got onboard, and while Clint and Fiona each grabbed a pole, Artie untied them from the dock and shoved the boat away.

"Push!" Fiona yelled.

She and Clint both pushed with their poles, getting the boat moving upriver, against the current. Clint was already looking forward to the trip being easier when they came back downriver.

No shots were fired from the dock, and nobody appeared to be concerned about their departure. Of course, that didn't mean someone couldn't have been watching from a hiding place.

"I'll take that," Artie said, grabbing the pole from Fiona. "You can eat your sandwich."

"Thank you, Artie," she said. "Think I should feed Clint?"

Artie shrugged.

"Why not?" he asked.

She grabbed the two remaining sandwiches and walked over to the other side of the boat, where Clint was putting his pole to use.

"Want me to feed you?"

"Sure, thanks."

She unwrapped the sandwiches, saw that they were both meat loaf.

"They had it left over from last night's supper," Artie yelled out.

"Good man!" Clint said.

Fiona held one out to Clint for him to take a bite, and then bit into her own. They ate them that way, as they got further and further from the dock.

Chapter Twenty-One

The first time they stopped poling, the current started to take them back downriver. Luckily, Fiona had remembered to buy an anchor. So when they wanted to take a rest, without going to shore, they dropped the anchor.

"How long is this trip going to take this way?" Clint asked them, as they passed a canteen back and forth.

"Eddie was talkin' about weeks," Artie said. "But he also talked about docking in Graybull for a while, before continuing on to the Little Bighorn River."

"Weeks on this boat?" Clint asked, alarmed. "There's got to be another way."

"Not according to Eddie," Artie told them. "He said it would be impossible to find the spot from land. It had to be from the river. Then it would be marked so it could be found from land."

Clint looked at Fiona, as if for help.

"Well," Fiona said, "Eddie and I did talk about something else."

"Like what?" Clint asked.

"Towing," she said. "If we could find a steamboat that was going upriver, maybe we could get them to tow us to the Little Bighorn. Then from there we could use the poles."

"Why didn't you tell me that before?" Clint asked.

She laughed.

"And miss the look on your face when Artie told you this might take weeks?"

"We can probably get to Warland on our own," Fiona said. "That's halfway to the mouth of the Little Bighorn. From there maybe we can get a tow."

"You really think so?" Artie asked.

"Well," she said. "I may have to use some feminine wiles, but . . ."

"If you do that," Artie said, "I'm sure we'll get towed."

"Then we should make that our plan," Clint suggested. "What do we say?"

"I say we get to the poles," Fiona said. "I'll take one for a while. One of you can rest."

"I'll take the other one, Clint," Artie said. "You take it easy for a while."

They pulled up the small anchor and got underway, again.

***

About an hour later Fiona stopped working her pole and shielded her eyes to look up ahead.

"Need a rest?" Clint asked.

"No," she said, "if I remember correctly, there's a bend in the river up ahead. It narrows there."

"So?" Artie asked.

"A perfect place for an ambush," Clint said.

"Exactly." She looked at him. "You're our marksman. You better be ready."

"I have a better idea," Clint said. "How close to shore can we get?"

"Very," she said. "It's a flat bottom boat, remember."

"So we can get close enough for me to wade ashore?" Clint asked.

"We can do that," she said. "We'll have to work against the tide a bit, but I think Artie's up to that. Aren't you, big man?"

"Just tell me how to do it."

"Okay," Fiona said, "here's what we have to do . . ."

***

When they had worked the boat close to shore Artie dug his pole in to hold it there against the current, and Fiona dropped the anchor overboard.

"Okay," Clint said. "Wait here. I'll wade ashore, then I'll move through the brush up ahead til I get to the bend."

"How will we know if you found anybody?" Fiona asked.

"You'll probably hear shots."

"And how will we know you're all right?"

"I'll be back," he said.

"And if you don't come back?"

He shrugged.

"Then I'm probably not all right."

Exasperated, she asked, "Then what do we do?"

"Decide between yourselves," Clint said. "Go back, forge ahead, or follow me and see what you find."

"That all makes sense," Artie said.

"Artie's wearing a gun," Clint said. "If you do follow me, stay close to him, Fiona."

"If I had a gun—"

"There's one in my saddlebag," Clint said, referring to his .32 Colt New Line. "It's small, but deadly. Take that."

"I will," she said, looking at Artie. "If anyone kills you, they'll have to deal with us, right, big man?"

"That's right," Artie agreed. "They will."

Chapter Twenty-Two

Clint waded ashore, carrying his gun belt on his shoulder and his boots in his hands. When he got there, he pulled on his boots and buckled on the belt. That done, he turned, waved to Artie and Fiona on the flatboat and headed upriver on foot.

He was aware that he might have been on the wrong side of the river. Or shooters could be set up on both sides. He probably should have brought his rifle, but he had left that on the boat for Artie, who said he was better with it than a handgun. If the river narrowed enough, Clint's pistol would be effective on either side.

As he moved through the brush along the river he watched the water, and the shore on the other side. He could see it getting closer. He also listened intently in case he was able to hear voices.

If there were men waiting to ambush them at the river bend, they were being quiet about it. He couldn't hear anyone or anything ahead. Finally, he heard a horse, so he knew he was getting close and that there was, indeed, an ambush.

He moved slowly, and as quietly as he could. Eventually, he spotted two men on his side of the river. They were leaning on rocks with rifles, watching the water.

Before he took care of them he had to determine if there were more, on either side of the river.

He circled around the two men, looking for more. He didn't see any on his side of the rushing water, so he started to pay attention to the other side. He didn't see anyone, but occasionally he caught a glint of sunlight off something shiny, like the barrel of a rifle. He decided if there were two men on his side of the river, there were probably two on the other side. Just to be safe, though, he decided to take these two without firing a shot, just in case there were more he hadn't seen. Then he could find out from them how many there were, total.

He got himself situated behind the men, close enough to hear them talking to each other.

"How much longer are we gonna have to wait?" one asked. He was on Clint's right.

"They said until the boat got here. It should be soon."

"Do we know who the people onboard are?" the first asked.

"We don't need to know," the second said. "Our job is to see they don't get any further than this bend in the river."

"By killin' them?"

"By firin' at them," the second man said, "from both sides of the river. We might drive them into the water, or capsize the boat—"

"It's a flatboat, right?" the first man asked "We ain't gonna capsize one of them by shootin' at it."

"Well then, we'll drive them into the water, and maybe blow the piss outta them," the first man said. "That's what we're gettin' paid to do."

Clint had heard enough. He came out of hiding, moved closer and announced his presence by saying, "I'll need you boys to drop your rifles and turn around."

The two men froze.

"And why would we do that?" the second man asked.

"Because I've got my gun on you, fellas," Clint said. He didn't remove his gun from his holster, but he reached down and very deliberately cocked it. He saw the first man, on his right, flinch.

"Rifles down, please," Clint said.

The two men each set their rifle down on the ground.

"Now stand with your hands raised."

"What's this about?" the second man asked.

"It's about keeping you from committing murder."

"That's crazy—"

"Just keep your hands raised and turn around."

Neither man was wearing a holster, but the second man must have had a pistol in his belt. As he turned around he drew with intentions of using it.

Clint drew and fired, drilling the man through the chest. His mouth fell open and he went down on his face.

"Jesus!" the other man said, flinching again. In his 20s, he was much younger than the other had been.

"You got a gun on you?" Clint asked.

"N-nossir!" the man gasped. "I—I only had my rifle."

"How many men are across the river?" Clint asked.

"Two."

"Armed with rifles?"

"Yessir."

Clint would have to get across the river to handle them, unless he knew exactly where they were.

"You're going to show me where they are."

"I-I don't know—"

"Yeah, you do," Clint said. "Move away from the rifles."

The young man did as he was told. Clint stepped up to the body, checked to make sure the man was dead, then took his pistol and rifle and threw them both into the river. He then picked up the younger man's rifle and held it.

"Show me where they are," he said.

"If I do, I-I'm dead."

"If you don't I'll kill you right now," Clint said. "If you do, I'll let you go and you can get a good head start."

The young man thought about it, then said, "All right, I'll show you."

Chapter Twenty-Three

"What do we do?" Fiona asked.

"It was only one shot," Artie pointed out.

"If it was a shot."

"Oh, it was," Artie said.

"Do you think he's all right?" she asked.

"I don't think Clint would ever be taken by one shot," Artie said. "But he can do a lot of damage with one. Yeah, I think he's all right."

"Then we should stay here?"

"We should," Artie said, "stay right here."

***

Clint got down behind the rocks the two men had been using. The other man moved next to him, as he had been with his partner.

"What's your name?"

"Pete."

"Don't forget, Pete," Clint told him, "if you try anything, I'll kill you."

"I understand."

"Show me where they are," Clint said. "Exactly."

"See that big tree, the one that looks like a hand reaching up to the sky?"

"What?"

"The branches, they look like they form a hand? Don't they? I mean, they do to me."

"Okay, I see a large tree, I don't see a hand . . . but keep going."

"To the left of the tree"

"Our left?" Clint asked.

"Right. There's a coupla rocks there. There's two men behind them."

"Do you know their names?"

"No, I don't," Pete said. "Um, Backlin—the man you killed—he did."

"So you and those other men were hired by Backlin?"

"That's right."

"And who hired Backlin?"

"I don't know," Pete said. "He just told us if we didn't do the job, they'd kill us."

"Okay," Clint said, sighting down the barrel of the rifle.

"Are you gonna kill 'em?" Pete asked.

"If I have to," Clint said. "But maybe I can just persuade them to give it up."

"You can kill 'em from here?"

"I can."

"Wow." Pete said, "that'd be some shootin'."

"You just sit still," Clint said. "How often do they stick their heads up?"

"Too often, Backlin said. He even threatened to shoot their heads off if he saw them. Only he wasn't that good a shot."

"Well, let's just take a look," Clint said.

He sighted down the barrel and figured to wait a good while. He only hoped Artie and Fiona wouldn't panic because of the single shot, and the fact that he didn't come back right away after it.

"There!" Pete said.

"Where?"

"The middle rock. See it? The top of his head."

"You've got sharp eyes," Clint said. "Yes, okay, I see."

A man's hat bobbed up every so often. And since it was only the hat, he decided to try something.

"Hold your breath, kid," Clint said.

The next time the hat popped up Clint fired, and the hat flew off.

A man stood up from behind the rock and yelled across the river. "That ain't funny!"

Clint fired again, hitting the man in the shoulder.

"Omigod!" Pete said. "You hit him both times."

"Well," Clint said, "the hat once, and him once."

"Did you kill 'im?"

"No," Clint said. "He'll be fine, as long as his friend gets him to a doctor."

"And if he doesn't?"

"Well then, he'll bleed out and die."

Clint kept his eyes on the rocks, and eventually saw one man helping another man as they staggered away from the rocks.

"And there they go," Clint said, looking at Pete. "Didn't have to kill either of them."

"Except for Backlin," Pete said, looking down at the body.

"Well," Clint said, "he asked for it."

"So n-now what? You gonna kill me?"

"Nope," Clint said. He threw the rifle he was holding into the river. "I'm going to leave you here. Do you have a horse nearby?"

"Yeah, we did," Pete said. "Left them off a ways so nobody would hear them."

"Well, you bury your partner, here, and then you can go."

"Go where?"

"Anywhere you want."

"I got no money. Backlin in was gonna pay us after."

"Well then," Clint said, "maybe he's got some money on him. You can check before you bury him."

"You mean . . . go through his pockets?"

"It's better than burying it with him, isn't it?" Clint asked.

***

Clint made his way back to the flatboat. When Fiona and Artie saw him they waved and he waved back.

"We only heard two shots," Artie said, "spaced pretty well apart. Didn't think we should act on 'em."

"Good thinking," Clint said. "I had to shoot two of the four men who were waiting for us, but it's all right to go on now."

"Really?" Fiona asked. "There were four men waitin' for us?"

"Yes, there were."

"Who hired them?"

"Unfortunately," Clint said, "I had to kill the only man who knew the answer to that."

"So what do we do now?" Fiona asked.

"We move on," Clint said. "I'll get on a pole."

"You just walked a long way, and shot two men," Fiona said. "We'll take the poles, you take a rest."

Clint didn't argue.

Chapter Twenty-Four

Because of the ambush, Artie suggested that when it was time to stop for the night over the next few days they do so in the center of the river, rather than taking the boat near shore.

"What about a steamboat running into us in the dark?" Clint asked.

"We should see any steamboat comin' in time to move, or signal," Artie said. "Besides, don't we wanna get a steamboat to tow us?"

"Tow us, yes," Fiona said, "smash into us, no."

"I think we're better off stopping near shore," Clint said. "Especially if the river's wide. How are they going to figure out where we are in order to ambush us again?" He looked at Fiona. "Does the river narrow, again?"

"Not the Bighorn," she said, "but the Little Bighorn does."

"Okay," Clint said, "we'll worry about that when we get to it."

So they camped each of the first three nights near shore, rather than take a chance of being run into by a steamboat in the center of the river. They started a fire each night, using a metal urn to hold the firewood, so that the flames never touched the actual wooden deck of the boat. They were able to make coffee and beans and keep the fire just high enough to generate some heat. As it happened, no steamboats passed after dark.

However, on the fourth day Clint ad Artie were on the poles while Fiona took a rest and drank some water. She was replacing the top of the canteen when she looked behind them and saw something.

"There's a steamboat coming," she called out.

"How far are we from Warland?" Clint asked.

"Probably a day," she replied.

"We wanted to get some supplies there, and then find a tow to Graybull," Clint reminded her.

"If we can get this boat to give us a tow," she said, "we could bypass Warland and go directly to Graybull. We can re-stock there."

Clint looked at Artie, who shrugged and said, "might as well let her give it a try."

"Okay, then," Clint said, "If you can get us a tow, go ahead and do it."

She stood up, unbuttoned her shirt at the top and pulled it down so that her shoulders, and upper slopes of her breasts showed.

"If that don't get 'em to stop," Artie said, "I don't know what will."

Chapter Twenty-Five

The steamboat slowed, seemed as if it was going to pass them by, but then came to a stop alongside. They could see the name, Sunny Jim written on the side.

"Havin' some trouble?" a man asked, looking down at them. Several other men were hanging over the side, trying to catch a look at Fiona.

"Actually, we're just a bit tired," Fiona said, fanning herself with one hand. "I wonder if we could get a tow?"

"Where are you headed?" the man asked.

"Graybull," she said.

"Let me talk to my Captain," the man said.

"Thank you so much," Fiona gushed.

As the man went to do that the other crew members talked among themselves, nudging each other, and one of them said, "You can come up here and ride with us."

"She's fine right here!" Artie roared back.

"Artie, Artie," Fiona said, so the men could hear her, "they're just bein' nice."

"Yeah," Artie said to Clint, "nice . . ."

"Relax," Clint said, so only Artie could hear him, "she knows what she's doing."

"I hope so," Artie said. "There's a whole crew on that boat. If they decide they want her, we're not gonna get in their way."

"Uh, yeah," Clint said, "we are."

"Madam!"

They all looked up and saw a man wearing a captain's hat looking down at them.

"Oh, hello, Captain," Fiona said. "Thank you so much for stopping to talk to us. You're too kind."

"Yes, well," the captain said, "I'm afraid that was my first mate's idea. Can you tell me what you and your friends are doin' here?"

"We have some business in Graybull," Clint said, thinking it might be time for him to speak up. "We thought the river might be the quickest way to get there."

"From where?" the Captain asked.

"Thermopolis."

"Well, you might have been right if you were on our boat," the captain said. "Look, I'd invite you onboard, but you can see the effect your lady friend is havin' on my men."

Clint waved a dismissive hand at the man.

"That's all right, Captain," Clint said. "We don't want to cause any trouble. If we could just get a tow to Graybull, that'd be good enough."

"Well," the captain said, "we have a stop in Warland. If that's not a problem for you we can do that, and then tow you to Graybull. Any further than that—"

"That's fine," Clint said. "We have business on the Little Bighorn after that."

"Ah, I see," the captain said. "Very well, then, that's where we'll part company."

"We appreciate it," Clint said.

"Yes," Fiona said, "you're too kind, sir."

"We'll throw you a rope," Sinclair called down. "Find some way to tie it up."

Since flatboats were often towed by steamboats, there was a metal hook on deck where they were able to tie the rope. The captain allowed the steamboat to move forward a bit, so that instead of alongside them it was directly in front. The crewmen were now hanging over the back rail.

"We're ready!" Clint shouted.

"Very well," the first mate called back. "Get back to work!" he shouted at the men.

As the crewmen disappeared from the rail, one of them threw a kiss at Fiona, and then the steamboat Sunny Jim began to move forward.

Chapter Twenty-Six

It was uncomfortable at first, being towed at high speed on the flatboat. The water kicked up at them, so they had to stand further back, and keep their oars and poles in so they wouldn't snap.

Artie wanted to eat, but he had to protect his food from getting soaked while he did.

By the time they reached Warland soaked to the skin, Fiona was attracting even more attention from the crew, as her clothing was sticking to her.

Once they stopped, Artie said, "I don't think we can stand that all the way to Graybull. Gettin' towed might not be such a good idea."

"Or," Clint said, "we can go ashore and buy some rain slickers, to keep us dry."

"Or," Fiona offered, "we could ask the captain to allow us onboard."

"You heard what he said about you and his men," Clint said. "That would only be looking for trouble."

"You know," she said, her hair plastered to her head, "if it was just me I'd get him to take me aboard and put me in his quarters."

"Why don't you do that?" Clint asked. "Artie and I will stay on the flatboat."

"No, no," she said, "I'll stick it out with you fellas. The slickers are a good idea."

"Let's go get them, then," Clint said.

"I think one of us should stay with the boat," Artie said. "Who knows if any of these crewmen will get curious? Or if the bushwhackers will find us, and sink it?"

"Good thinking," Clint said. "I can stay—"

"You're the money man," Artie said. "You go to the store with Fiona, and I'll stay here."

"I'll leave you my rifle," Clint said.

"I have my gun." Artie patted his pistol, which was tucked into his belt.

"I'll leave it, anyway," Clint said. "And we'll bring you some dry clothes."

"Thanks," Artie said, and then called out, "just make sure they're big!"

Clint and Fiona waved and climbed up onto the dock, with Clint giving her a boost.

They asked a man on the dock where the nearest mercantile was, and he gave them directions while staring at Fiona's attributes, which were starkly on display in her wet clothes.

When they got to the mercantile Fiona first found some dry clothing for herself and asked the clerk if she could change somewhere.

"Of course, Ma'am," he said. "In the back."

"Thank you."

"Sir?" the clerk said, trying hard not to watch Fiona walk away. Her behind was perfectly formed and on display in her wet trousers.

"Do you have rain slickers?"

"Oh, yes sir," the young man said, "we have many..."

***

By the time Fiona came out in her dry shirt and trousers, and the boots she had taken the time to dry off, as well, Clint was at the counter, settling up.

"Shirts, slickers," the clerk said. "Five dollars and twenty-five cents, sir."

Clint paid, turned to face Fiona as the clerk wrapped the purchases.

"How do I look?" she asked, doing a twirl.

"Decent."

Her face fell.

"That's all?"

"I mean," he said, "dry. Your clothes aren't sticking to you."

"I know," she said. "It feels great. I only wish I had time for a bath."

"You want to get wet again?"

"It's a different kind of wet, isn't it?" she asked.

"Yes, it is," Clint said. "Come on, let's get back. The captain said they'd only be docked long enough to offload a few things."

"Right."

They left the store and headed back to the dock. Ahead of them, coming their way, were four men, dressed like crewmen. When the men saw them one smiled and nudged the others, pointing.

"There's our lady friend," he said, when they came within earshot.

"Hello, boys."

Clint and Fiona tried to continue walking, but the four crewmen blocked their way.

"Don't you wanna introduce yerself?" the first man asked. "I mean, we are towin' you to where you wanna go."

"I'll be happy to introduce myself," she said, "to your captain."

"The Captain's an ol' geezer," the first man said. "You wanna meet young men, like us."

They were all in their 30s and 40s, rough looking men who knew nothing about how to act with a woman.

"I think you boys better get on with what you were doing," Clint said.

The four men exchanged glances, and grinned.

"Why don't you just leave the lady with us," one man said, "just go and do what you were gonna do. Huh?"

"I don't think the lady wants to go with you," Clint said.

"Why don't you let her decide?"

"He's right," she said, "I'm not interested."

"You won't even give us a chance?" one of the other men said.

"I don't like your manners," she said. "My friend and I would like to get back to our boat."

"And you better get back to yours," Clint said, "before it leaves without you."

"We wuz gonna get a drink first," the first man said. "Come with us."

"No," she said.

"Now look—" the man said, reaching out for her.

She swatted his hand away.

"What the—" He reached again, this time she punched him square in the nose.

"You bitch!"

"You asked for it," Clint said.

"Get 'er!" he told the others.

"Before you do that," Fiona said, "let me introduce my friend, Mr. Clint Adams."

The three men froze.

"Adams?"

"That's right," Fiona said.

They exchanged a glance, and one said, "I thought he was dime novel stuff."

"No," Fiona said, "he's not. He's the Gunsmith."

"Jesus," the first man said, still holding his nose.

"No harm done here," Clint said, "except for your nose, and you asked for that. Now should we all get back?"

"Yeah, yeah," one of the other men said, "we better get back."

The four men turned and hurried away.

"I hope you don't mind I did that," Fiona said. "I was just trying to avoid trouble."

"No problem," he said. "It worked, didn't it?"

"Looks like it," she said, "for now. I just hope it keeps working."

Chapter Twenty-Seven

"There you are!" Artie shouted. "They're gettin' ready to—whatayacallit? —shove off."

"We're here," Clint said.

Artie helped Fiona get aboard, then accepted the packages from Clint.

"Slickers, and a shirt for you."

"What about food?"

"We'll do that in Graybull."

Artie stripped off his shirt and put on his dry one.

"Are you ready down there?" someone shouted to them. "We're getting ready to cast off."

"We're ready," Clint said.

"We'll be in Graybull by nightfall," the man shouted.

"That sounds good," Clint said. He turned to Artie and Fiona. "Slickers on."

They put them on just as the Sunny Jim started to pull away from the dock.

"Here we go!" Clint said.

"When we get to Graybull," Fiona said, "I'm taking a bath!"

They took their positions on the boat.

***

About two hours later the steamboat started to slow down visibly, and then stop. The flatboat bumped into the stern.

"What's going on?" Fiona wondered.

"I don't know," Clint said.

"These slickers were a good idea," Artie said. "I'm dry underneath."

"That's good," Clint said. "I don't know why we're stopped, but if you want something to eat, Artie, you better get to it."

Abruptly, the captain appeared, looking down at them.

"I understand you're Clint Adams," he said.

"That's right," Clint said. "Is that a problem?"

"Would you come aboard so we can talk?"

"If you insist."

"It's a request," the captain said.

"Okay, then, how do I do that?"

"We'll throw down a rope ladder."

A few moments later, the ladder appeared, unfurling its way down.

"If your friends want to come aboard, too, they're welcome."

Clint looked at them.

Fiona shrugged and said, "I'm fine here."

"I'll stay with Fiona," Artie said.

"Okay," Clint said. "I'll be back soon . . . hopefully."

He climbed unsteadily up the rope ladder, until he was standing next to a portly man with a dour expression, wearing a captain's hat.

"My name is Captain James Sinclair." They shook hands.

"Wait," Clint said. "You're Sunny Jim?"

"That's right," the captain said. "This is my boat. I'm the captain, and the owner. Come with me, please?"

Clint followed the captain across the deck to the pilot house, while crewmen stared after them. He saw the four men he and Fiona had faced in the street. One of them had a swollen nose.

When they entered the pilot house the man at the wheel looked at the captain. He was only about 5 1/2 feet tall, but Clint could see the strength in his arms.

"This is my pilot, Danny."

"Hello," Danny said, without taking his eyes off the river.

"Danny, this is Clint Adams," the Captain said, "also known as the Gunsmith."

Danny frowned.

"I thought that was just a legend."

The captain looked at Clint.

"Maybe it is," he said. "Are you a legend, Mr. Adams?"

"Not in my mind, Captain," Clint said. "Can you tell me why I'm here?"

"No, I can't," Captain Sinclair said. "That's what I want you to tell me."

"I'm sorry?"

"A man like you doesn't just happen to be on this river in a flatboat," the captain said. "What brings you here?"

"Does being towed the rest of the way depend on my answer to that question?" Clint asked.

"No, of course not," the Captain said. "Let's just call it an old man's curiosity."

"You're not that old," Clint said. "There's more behind this than idle curiosity."

"Humor me," the Captain said.

Clint studied the man, then said, "No, I don't think I will, Captain. What I'm doing here is my business."

Sinclair frowned, looked out at the river for a few moments before speaking again.

"All right, then," he said, "what if being towed the rest of the way did depend on your answering that question?"

"Then I'd say let me get back on my boat and you can cut us loose," Clint answered. "We'll make our way alone from here."

"Okay," the captain said, "let me ask a more direct question."

"Go ahead."

"Does your presence here have anything to do with three hundred and fifty thousand dollars in gold?"

"What?" Clint asked, feigning confusion. "What the hell are you talking about?"

"Oh, come now, Mr. Adams," the captain said. "Are you gonna tell me you know nothing about the treasure of the Little Bighorn?"

"What treasure?"

"So you're not looking for the treasure."

"You just told me about it," Clint said. "Maybe I'll look for it now. Where would I look?"

"If I knew I wouldn't tell you."

"But if I knew you thought I'd tell you, huh?" Clint asked.

"Well, seeing as I have a bigger boat than you, I thought we might make a deal."

"What kind of deal?"

"We use my boat and your knowledge. We find the treasure and transport it on the Sunny Jim."

"This treasure," Clint said, still playing dumb. "How heavy is it?"

"Very," the Captain said. "You're not gonna get it on that flatboat. You'll sink."

"Well then, I guess I won't be looking for it after all," Clint said. "I don't want to sink."

Captain Sinclair looked over at his pilot, who kept his eyes straight ahead.

"Think it over," he said, then.

"What if I did find the treasure, Captain?" Clint asked, "How many of your crew would I be splitting with?"

"You let me worry about the crew," Sinclair said. "You and me split fifty-fifty."

"And what about my two friends?"

"You pay them out of your half, I'll take care of my crew out of mine. There should be plenty to go around."

"Well, I tell you what," Clint said. "If I find a treasure along the way, I'll give your offer some thought."

"You do that," Captain Sinclair said. "Let's get you back down that ladder. That is, unless you and your friends want to ride up here with us."

"No, that's okay," Clint said. "We'll be in Graybull tonight. That'll make all the difference. We can ride our flatboat until then."

"As you wish."

***

Clint climbed down the shaky ladder and rejoined Artie and Fiona. Somebody on the boat pulled the ladder up.

"So what was all that about?" Fiona asked.

Clint told them about Sinclair's questions.

"So he's lookin' for the treasure?" Artie asked.

"I'm not sure," Clint said. "He knows about it, and thinks we're looking for it. That's as much as I know."

The steamboat began to move and they were underway, again.

"We'll talk about this when we get to Graybull," Clint said, and they donned their slickers.

Chapter Twenty-Eight

It was almost dark when they reached Graybull. The steamboat slowed, then stopped, allowing the flatboat to bump into it's stern. From there they used the poles to get themselves to the dock, where Artie tied them off.

"Finally," Fiona said, when they were on the dock. "Can we get something to eat?"

"Definitely," Artie said.

"I think we should get hotel rooms," Clint said. "And a good night's sleep tonight."

"Sounds good to me," Fiona said.

"Me, too."

"Let's go, then," Clint said.

"What about the supplies on the boat?" Fiona asked.

"We'll just take my saddlebags and our weapons," Clint said. "There's nothing else worth anything."

"The slickers," Artie said. "We might need them, again."

"Okay, yeah," Clint said. "We'll take them along, too."

They gathered the things from the flatboat and started away from the docks. Graybull was a larger town than Thermopolis, with more choices of hotels.

"Why don't we just take the nearest one to the docks?" Artie suggested.

But the hotel that was the closest was a dilapidated wreck.

"How about the closest decent hotel?" Fiona asked.

"Good thinking," Clint said.

***

They found what they were looking for and got three rooms.

"I'm goin' to my room and lie down," Artie said, and went up the stairs ahead of them.

Clint walked Fiona up to the second floor.

"We only needed two rooms, you know," she said.

"Not a chance," Clint said. "Artie snores like a bull."

"I didn't mean you and Artie sharing a room," she told him.

"I know what you meant, Fiona," he said, and left her standing at her door.

When Clint got inside his room he dropped his saddlebags and rifle into a corner, and realized that Artie had the right idea. He dropped onto the bed without even removing his boots and fell asleep.

***

Clint was awakened by a knock at his door. He hoped it wasn't Fiona with carnal intentions. He was still too worn out.

He went to the door with his gun in hand and asked. "Who is it?"

"Sheriff Dan Peters," a man's voice said. "Can you open the door, please, Mr. Adams."

Clint opened the door enough to see a badge, then opened it the rest of the way.

"Sheriff," he said. "what can I do for you?"

"Well, first you can let me in and second, you can holster that gun."

"Sorry," Clint said, walking to the bedpost to holster the gun, "force of habit."

The sheriff closed the door.

"What can I do for you, Sheriff?" Clint asked.

"I heard you were in town," the lawman said. "And I heard that you're looking for the treasure of the Little Bighorn."

"Not you, too," Clint said. "Who told you that?"

"I won't reveal my source," the lawman said. "But what's the Gunsmith doing in Graybull if not searching for the treasure?"

"Maybe I won't reveal anything to you, either," Clint said. "Let's just say I'm passing through."

"On a flatboat?"

"Do you know another way to get up and down the river?" Clint asked.

"It just doesn't make sense," the sheriff said. "For the Gunsmith."

"You don't have any idea what makes sense for me, and what doesn't," Clint said.

"Well," the sheriff said, "maybe I'll just find out on my own."

"You do that," Clint said. "Now, if you don't mind, I want to get back to my sleep."

"We'll talk again, soon," Sheriff Peters said, and left the room.

Clint went back to the bed and sat, but getting any sleep was out of the question. Who else could be the sheriff's source except Captain "Sunny Jim" Sinclair? And, if not him, then too many people were thinking Clint was after the Bighorn treasure.

He wondered if the sheriff had also talked with Fiona and Artie, so he decided to go down the hall and find out.

He went to Fiona's room first. She answered at his first knock, looking lovely and fresh from a bath.

"There you are," she said. "I thought you were going to sleep all day. Come in."

"I didn't have a bath to wake me up," he said. "Maybe I should."

"Well, come in," she said, "and we'll talk about it."

"Not a chance," he said. "Did the local sheriff come and talk to you?"

"The sheriff?" She frowned. "No, why would he?"

"He woke me to ask if I was looking for the treasure." Her frown deepened.

"That's not good. Too many people seem to know what we're up to."

"Or they know what I'm up to," Clint said.

"Do you think the captain was involved in trying to ambush us?" she asked.

"No."

"Then two different factions suspect what we're do-ing," she said. "Who told the sheriff?"

"That's what I'd like to find out."

"Did the sheriff talk to Artie?"

"I'm going to find out right now," he said.

"I'll come along—"

"No," Clint said, "you smell too good, right now. I want Artie to concentrate. Stay here and I'll let you know."

"Come back soon," she said. "I'll still be smelling good."

Chapter Twenty-Nine

Clint had to knock twice before Artie answered. He was bootless and shirtless when he answered the door.

"Come on in," he said.

"Sorry to wake you."

"You ain't the only one," Artie said. "The local law was here."

"Sheriff Peters?"

"You, too?" Artie asked, sitting on the bed. "Did he ask about the treasure?"

"He did."

"Who sent him, do you think?" Artie asked. "That steamboat Captain?"

"I don't know," Clint said. "He wouldn't say."

"He didn't tell me, neither."

"Why don't you go back to sleep?" Clint suggested.

"What're you gonna do?"

"Have a bath."

"You're gonna get wet, again?" Artie asked. "Ain't you had enough?"

Clint smiled.

"It's a different kind of wet."

***

Clint went down to the lobby to arrange for a hot bath but didn't spend as much time soaking in it as he might have. He felt too vulnerable there, and who knew if whoever was behind the attempted ambush might try again? As always, he kept his gun close by.

After the bath he felt better—at least, physically. Well enough to be hungry, and he knew Artie would be, as well. Probably Fiona. He went back up to the second floor to fetch them both.

"Hungry?" Fiona asked, when she answered her door. "Starved, is more like it."

"Let's get Artie and go find someplace," he said.

They walked down to Artie's door and pounded on it for about five minutes before admitting he wasn't asleep, he just wasn't there.

"Or?" Fiona said.

"Shit," Clint said, and forced the door.

The room was empty.

"Okay, that's good," Fiona said. "He probably went out to eat without waiting for us."

"Maybe we'll run into him," Clint said. "he wouldn't go too far, probably stopped into the first place he saw."

They left the hotel and started walking, confident they'd find Artie in the first restaurant they came to, unless he had walked in the opposite direction. But they figured he'd walk away from the river, as they were doing.

"How about there?" Fiona asked, pointing across the street.

It was a café with a clean storefront, which was encouraging.

"Good as any," Clint said.

They crossed the street and entered, immediately saw Artie Small seated at a back table, with plates of food in front of him. He saw them and waved. They walked to his table.

"Sit," he said. "I'll make room."

They looked at all the plates on the table and Clint said, "That's okay. We'll sit over here."

They moved to the very next table and sat down. Both tables were set against the back wall. Artie had learned his lesson from Clint.

A waiter came over and took their orders, both for beef stew. They wanted something warm inside. Even after a hot bath, and even though the weather was mild, Clint still seemed to feel a chill from the river.

Artie seemed to have the same idea, but in addition to a bowl of stew he had a steak platter in front of him, and a basket of biscuits.

"Did the sheriff talk to Artie?" Fiona asked, while they drank coffee and waited for their food.

"He did."

"I wonder why he didn't talk to me?"

"Maybe he doesn't think you're a full partner," Clint pointed out.

"Just a girl along for the ride?" she said. "Your girl, or Artie's?"

"Maybe."

"I should go talk to him," she said, "show him where he's wrong."

"Probably not," Clint said. "Let him keep guessing."

"Does he know who you are?"

"Yes," Clint said. "He pointed it out."

"Maybe that's all he cares about," Fiona offered. "He doesn't want you to kill anyone while you're in town."

"He mentioned the treasure."

"Damn," she said. "I wonder how much talking Eddie did about it?"

"Well," Clint said, "he recruited you, and Artie. Maybe he tried recruiting others."

"And he ends up dead."

The waiter came with their food and they suspended their conversation while they ate.

Chapter Thirty

When they had finished eating and all their plates were cleared—especially Artie's—the big man moved to their table and they had coffee and pie together.

"Sorry," Artie said, "but I woke up starving and I couldn't wait. I stopped at the first place I saw, and figured you'd do the same."

"It worked out," Clint said.

"So did the lawman talk to you?" he asked Fiona.

"No," she said. "Clint and I talked about that. He probably thinks I'm just a . . . girlfriend."

"Whose?" Artie asked.

"It doesn't matter," Fiona said, and the big man nodded. "We just figure we'll keep him in the dark about me."

"Fine," Artie said.

"Did he ask you about the treasure?" she asked.

"Yeah, he did. I played dumb."

"That's good," Clint said.

"So what do we do now?" Fiona asked.

"Well," Clint said, "we're going to head up the Little Bighorn."

"On our own?" Fiona asked.

"We can't rely on Sunny Jim to tow us any further," Clint said, "not with Captain Sinclair on the lookout for treasure."

"What about another steamboat?" Artie asked.

"Let's not count on anything but ourselves," Clint suggested. "And then we'll see where we go from there."

"I agree with Clint."

"Okay, then," Artie said. "We head out again in the mornin'?"

"We do," Clint said. "After we pick up some provisions. But let's stay in the hotel tonight."

"I was kinda hopin' to stop in a saloon," Artie said.

"So far the captain has asked us about the treasure, and then the sheriff. Who knows who else is out there wondering? And what about whoever shot Eddie Lee? Why take a chance?"

"I could use a drink, myself," Fiona said. "How about one trip to a saloon?"

They both looked at Clint with hopeful eyes.

"Well, it's early," Clint said. "Why don't we buy the supplies, arrange to pick them up in the morning, then spend some time in our rooms before we go out for supper and a drink?"

"Sounds good to me," Fiona said. "Artie?"

Artie didn't look happy.

"I didn't hear anything in there," he said, "about lunch."

***

They walked from the café to the mercantile and did the shopping together. At one point, while Artie and Fiona were arguing about the benefit of canned fruit, Clint looked out the window and saw the sheriff across the street. The lawman seemed to have his eyes on the mercantile.

"What is it?" Fiona asked, coming up alongside him.

"The sheriff," Clint said, "he's across the street."

"Watching us?"

"I don't know," Clint said. "Maybe he's just watching the store."

"Why?"

"I don't know," Clint said. "We'll find out when we leave."

Clint turned and walked to the counter, since he was paying for the supplies.

"We'll pick them up first thing in the morning," Clint said.

"We could deliver them, if you like," the middle-aged clerk said.

"That would work, too."

"Where?" the clerk asked.

"The dock," Clint said. "We have a flatboat."

"Just be there," the clerk said, "so that my men know where to load."

"We'll be there," Clint promised.

As they started to leave, Clint and Fiona told Artie about the lawman out front.

"Let's find out if he's watching us."

"How do we do that?" Artie asked.

"Easy," she said. "If he stops watching the store after we leave, he's watching us."

"I have a better idea," Clint said.

"What?" Fiona asked.

"Let's find out if he's watching me," Clint said.

"Why don't you think he's watching me?" Fiona asked.

"I'd be watchin' you," Artie said. "I mean, between the three of us."

"Thank you, Artie."

"If he's watching you, Fiona," Clint said, "or Artie, we're about to find out."

"What do we do?" Artie asked.

"We split up," Clint said.

"But you said you wanted us to stay together," Artie said.

"Right," Clint said. "We'll split up and meet back at our hotel. And we'll see which one of us he follows there."

"My money's on Fiona," Artie said.

"I appreciate that, big guy," Fiona said, "but I think it's Clint."

They stepped outside the mercantile and, from there, they split up and went in three different directions.

Chapter Thirty-One

Clint went to the right, started walking at a brisk pace. He turned the next corner and managed to look over his shoulder at the same time. Sure enough, the sheriff was pacing him while remaining on the other side of the street.

He kept walking.

***

When he reached the hotel Fiona and Artie were sitting in chairs out front.

"Looks like you were right," Fiona said. "He's right behind you."

There was an empty chair, so Clint sat with them.

"What do you think he wants?" Artie asked.

"Might just be what every lawman wants," Clint said. "To be around when I get shot."

"That's horrible," Fiona said.

"Or," Clint said, "he might be interested in treasure."

"I'm gonna go upstairs and take a nap," Artie said, getting up from his chair. "Come and get me when it's time to eat."

"Sleep tight," Fiona said.

As Artie went into the hotel, the sheriff stepped into the street and started across.

"Here he comes," Fiona said.

"Let's hear what he has to say," Clint said, "then we'll know if it's the treasure he's interested in, or me."

The sheriff reached them and stopped short of stepping up onto the boardwalk.

"I guess you're wonderin' why I've been watchin' you," Sheriff Peters said.

"Watching who?" Fiona asked. "Watching me?"

"Watching all of you, in fact," Peters said. "Strangers comin' to Graybull are usually bringin' trouble with them."

"Why do you think that is?" Fiona asked.

"I don't think," he said, "I know. It's because we're near the mouth of the Little Bighorn River, where people go to look for that treasure."

"What treasure?" Clint asked.

"Look," Peters said, "all I'm tellin' you is to be on the lookout. You're not the only ones lookin' for it. And people will do anythin' to find it. So stay together and watch each other's back."

"And what will you be doing?" Fiona asked.

"I'm always on the lookout for trouble," Peters said, then looked directly at Clint. "And you being who you are could make it a helluva lot worse."

"Well, we appreciate you looking out for us, Sheriff," Fiona said.

"Oh, I'm not lookin' out for you," the lawman said. "I'm just lookin' out for my town."

"Just doing your job," Clint said.

"That's about the size of it."

"Well, thanks for the warning," Clint said. "Is there anything else you'd like to tell us?"

"No, I've just got to get on with my rounds," the lawman said.

"Don't let us keep you," Fiona replied.

Peters touched the brim of his hat, turned and headed up the street.

"Do you think he's interested in the treasure, himself?" Fiona asked.

"Well now," Clint said, "that's a good question. Three hundred and fifty thousand dollars in gold would certainly appeal to a man who's making forty a month."

"It would appeal to any man," Fiona said, "or woman."

"We're going to have to keep an eye on him," Clint said, "while we keep an eye on everybody else around us."

"Great," Fiona said, "nothing like being alert all the time for somebody who might be out to kill you."

"Tell me about it."

"Oh, I'm sorry," she said. "I know that's the way you have to live all the time. I can't imagine it."

"Hopefully, you won't have to do it for very long," he said.

"Maybe," she said, "you can help me keep my mind off it, then?"

Chapter Thirty-Two

As the door to Fiona's room closed on them, Clint and Fiona went into a longtime coming clinch. In a fevered frenzy they removed each other's clothing and fell onto the bed, Clint's hard cock pressed firmly between their hot bodies.

"I've been needing this for a long time," she said, reaching down and grasping him.

"You say the nicest things."

"I do nice things, too," she said. "Like this."

She pushed him onto his back, slithered down and quickly took his penis into her hot mouth. Sucking him avidly, she slid her hands beneath him to cup his buttocks, her head bobbing up and down.

"Jesus," he said.

"Nice?" she asked, letting him pop out of her mouth.

"More than nice."

"Good."

She took him back inside and continued to suck on him. He hadn't realized it, but he needed this, too, to release some of the pent up pressure of hunting for treasure while possibly being hunted, themselves. Also, he wouldn't have admitted it to anyone, but being towed by the steamboat was a harrowing experience. He was secretly hoping they could make their own way up the Little Bighorn.

But that was something they would talk about later, when he wasn't in her mouth. He reached with both hands to cup the back of her head.

She sucked him until he was scant seconds from exploding in her mouth, and then released him and took firm hold of him, with her fingers wrapped around the base of his cock.

"Christ," he said, as she managed to stem the tide, "your turn now."

"Yes!" she said, falling onto her back next to him. "Go ahead, make me a happy woman."

"My pleasure," he said, kissing his way down her body, momentarily skipping her crotch to pepper her lovely thighs, and then going back to the task at hand—making the lady happy.

He pressed his mouth to her fragrant pussy, found it already wet and waiting for him. He attacked her with his mouth and tongue, causing her to arch her back and lift her butt up off the bed, pressing it firmly against him. But he placed his elbows on her thighs, pressing her back down to the bed, and kept her pinned there while he continued to work on her, bringing her closer and closer to completion. Being pinned down, despite being a powerful woman, seemed to make the experience intensify.

As she went into spasms of pleasure that rocked her body, Clint immediately mounted her and drove his hard cock into her hot depths. Her eyes went wide, because new waves of pleasure mixed with the old and her eyes actually began to water.

Clint pounded into her. As much as she needed this, he needed it, too. He grabbed her ankles, spread her wide and just kept ramming himself in and out of her until they were both grunting from the effort. Once again, as the last time, Artie was in a room down the hall, but this time Clint wasn't worrying about whether or not the big man could hear them. He was only thinking about one thing, and that was his own release.

"Oh God, yeah." Fiona was finally able to form words. Or one word. She kept saying "Yeah, yeah, yeah, yeah," as he pounded into her, again and again.

Finally, he stopped, jamming himself deep inside of her and exploding, so that she felt like thousands of little needles of pleasure were filling her up.

He released her ankles so that her legs fell to the mattress, and he laid down beside her.

"Oh my God," she said. "I've never been manhandled like that."

"Sorry," he said, "but I needed that."

"Don't be sorry," she said, "I needed that, too. I only hope Artie didn't hear us."

"I didn't even think about that," Clint said.

"We'll have to get ourselves cleaned up and then collect him for supper," she said. "I think if we get him a big steak, everything will be all right."

"He does like to eat," Clint said.

"But," she said, reaching over and stroking his still semi-hard erection, "we do still have some time."

He enjoyed the way her hand was not only stroking him, but stoking the fire inside him, again.

"Mmm," she said, running her mouth over his chest and nipples while continuing to work his cock, "it looks like you have some interest."

"It looks like you're doing your best to make me rise to the occasion," he observed.

She slid down between his legs and took a long lick of his cock.

"Mmm," she said, "tasty. Maybe from being inside me?" She flicked her tongue over him again, catching him just beneath the spongy head, making him jump.

"You're pretty tasty, yourself," he admitted.

She sucked him into her mouth again, then let him slide free, shiny with her saliva.

"So are you," she said, "with no help from me."

Chapter Thirty-Three

Five men rode into town just as Fiona was finishing Clint off for a second time.

"What now?" Frank Johnson asked. "Now that we're in this dead end river town?"

"Now you go down to the docks and check to see if their boat is there," Sam Train said.

"And if it is?" Johnson asked.

"Then we have them," Train said.

"And what do we do with them?" Alex Maxwell asked. "Kill 'em?"

"You mean like you killed Ed Lee?" Train asked. "Before we got any useful information out of him?"

"That was his own fault," Maxwell said. "I had to shoot him."

"In the back?" Train asked.

"Look, lemme tell you—"

"Never mind," Train said. "You go with Frank, find out if that flatboat is on the docks. After that we'll decide what to do."

"They've already killed some of our men," Maxwell pointed out.

"So you and Frank have to make sure you don't get killed," Train said. "Meet us in a saloon after?"

"Which saloon?" Johnson asked.

"The one nearest the docks," Train said. "Now go!"

The two men rode away, and the other three went in search of that saloon.

***

The Broken Oar Saloon was the closest to the docks, so it served both cowboys and crewmen. Sam Train and his men walked in, stopped just inside the batwings and looked around.

"Fuckin' sailors," Red Cardwell groused.

Train looked at the bar, saw some men in western garb, while the men wearing crewmen's clothes were seated at tables.

"The bar," he said, and led the way.

There was room for the three of them, but they deliberately fanned out to take even more. The other men at the bar moved away and gave them room, as they were obviously ready for trouble.

"Three beers," Train said to the bartender.

The bartender obeyed immediately, recognizing trouble when he saw it.

"This place is a dump," Cardwell said.

The other man, Lew Hastings, sipped the beer and said, "At least the beer's cold."

The two men argued about what made a saloon good or bad, but Sam Train ignored them, preferring, instead, to think about $350,000 in gold.

***

Clint and Fiona walked down the hall and knocked on Artie's door. The big man answered immediately.

"About time," he said. "I'm starvin'!"

"You're always starving," Clint said.

"Let's go," Fiona said. "We can ask somebody where to get a good steak."

"I should've asked the sheriff," Clint said, as they walked down the stairs. "Gotten some use out of him."

"I'll ask the desk clerk," Fiona said. "They're always very helpful."

"I wonder why," Clint said.

When they reached the lobby Fiona went to the desk clerk, who stared at her, starry-eyed, while she asked the question. Moments later she came over to Clint and Artie.

"He was very nice and recommended a place down the street."

They left the hotel and followed the clerk's directions to a restaurant with large front windows, high ceiling and bare wooden floors that looked stained—hopefully from food.

"Here?" Clint asked.

"Why not?" Artie asked. "Smells good."

Clint looked around. No one outside was watching them, and everyone inside—about half the tables were full—was paying attention to their food.

"They all look happy with their food," Artie said.

Clint looked at Fiona, who shrugged and asked, "Why not? We're all hungry."

"Okay," Clint said, giving in, "let's try it."

They went inside. Clint didn't like the large windows, so they found a table not only against a wall, but off to the side so they couldn't be seen from outside.

A bored looking waiter with a heavily stained apron came over and asked what they wanted.

"Three steak dinners," Artie said, "and three mugs of beer."

"Gotcha," the waiter said.

"This is gonna be good," Artie said. "I can feel it."

Clint had his doubts, but when the steaks came he had to admit they were expertly cooked. And the beer was cold.

"Well?" Artie asked, in the midst of a huge bite.

"It's going to depend on the coffee," Clint said.

Not only was the coffee good and strong, but they had the best peach pie he had ever eaten.

"They're just going to have to clean up a bit in here," Clint said, as they went out the door.

"It has character," Fiona said.

"And if they cleaned all the stains off the floor, the food probably wouldn't taste the same," Artie said.

"It's probably blood," Fiona said.

"Cow's blood," Artie added, with a smile. "The best kind."

Chapter Thirty-Four

By the time Maxwell and Johnson got to the Broken Oar, Train and the others had imbibed a lot of beer.

"It's about time!" Train roared, lifting his glass to them. "Come on. You have some catchin' up to do." He looked at the bartender. "Five beers!"

The bartender set them up. There were no other men at the bar. It had been left to Sam Train and his men, who were obviously gun hands.

Maxwell and Johnson accepted their beers and quenched their thirst before speaking.

"The flatboat is there," Johnson said.

Train put his hand on the man's shoulder.

"And is it theirs?"

"We were told two men and a woman got off of it," Maxwell said. "A large man, and a tall woman."

"And the Gunsmith," Johnson added.

"So they know him here."

"They do," Johnson said.

Train turned and looked at the men who were seated at tables.

"Everybody out!" he shouted.

They looked at him, shocked.

"Did you hear him?" Hastings shouted, and the four gunmen turned to face the patrons. "Out! While you can still walk!"

The crewmen were the first to stand and leave, for they were not armed. Then, after they had gone, the others filed out, slowly, reluctantly. Some of them were wearing guns, and might have wanted to resist, but in the end the saloon was emptied of all but Sam Train, his men and the bartender.

"And you," Train said to the barkeep. "Just keep pourin'."

He turned back to his four men.

"So what do we do now?" Cardwell asked.

"We find 'em," Train said, "follow 'em, kill 'em, and get rich."

"Simple," Maxwell said, with a smile.

***

While the plan had been to stay away from saloons, Artie told Clint he was going to one.

"You can come or not," he said, "but I ain't hidin' in my room, no more."

Clint looked at Fiona.

"Ohm, not me," she said. "The last thing I want is to be around a bunch of drunk men. I'll go to my room and see you fellas in the morning."

"Early," Clint said.

"Of course."

They walked Fiona to the hotel, then went off down the street in search of a saloon. They found one only two blocks away, called The Bighorn Saloon.

"Not much imagination there," Clint said.

"Huh?" Artie said. "Makes sense to me."

"Right."

They went inside, found it very crowded at that time of the day. It looked like people from town mixed with the men from the docks.

They went to the bar where Artie elbowed them some room. A couple of men turned to glare at him, but faced with his size, they backed off.

"Two beers," Clint ordered.

"Comin' up."

They looked around, saw no gaming going on, but there were girls working the floor. Up front was a small stage, indicating they sometimes had musical entertainment.

"Here ya are," the bartender said.

"How much?" Clint asked.

"No charge."

"Why?"

The bartender pointed down to the end of the bar, Where Sheriff Peters raised his mug to them.

"Tell the sheriff we thank him," Clint said. "And ask him to come over and drink with us."

"Yessir."

The bartender delivered the message, and Peters moved down and stood with them.

"What's on your mind, Sheriff?" Clint asked.

"Can't a man just be friendly?" Peters asked.

"He could, but why do I think it's something else?"

"Well," Peters said, "I just thought you'd like to know that some men came to town askin' about your flatboat."

"Is that right? How many?"

"Five," Peters said. "Two went to the dock to ask questions, the other three went to the Broken Oar Saloon. I'm pretty sure they're all there, now."

"You tellin' us this so we can go over there?" Artie asked.

"The opposite," Peters said. "I'm tellin' you so you can stay away from them."

"Not much chance of that," Artie said. "If they know where our flatboat is, they'll be watching."

"But that's all they'll be doing," Clint pointed out. "Watching, waiting for us to find what they're looking for."

"Treasure," Peters said.

Clint looked at the lawman.

"Which we know absolutely nothing about," he said.

"Of course," Sheriff Peters said.

Chapter Thirty-Five

Sam Train sat in the Broken Oar with 4 of his men while the 5th, Hastings, went to the nearest hotel and got them rooms—a room for Train, and then several the others could share.

"Sam, you sure we shouldn't just grab the woman and make Adams and the other man tell us where the treasure is?" Maxwell asked.

"No, we shouldn't," Train said.

"Why not?" Maxwell asked.

"Because they don't know, stupid. They were gonna depend on Ed Lee to get them to it."

"And you killed him," Johnson pointed out, with a smile.

"Shut up!" Maxwell said. He looked at Train. "So if they was gonna depend on Lee, how they gonna find it, now?"

"I don't know," Train said, "but they still got a better chance of findin' it than we do."

"So we don't grab the woman," Johnson said, "Too bad. She looks real tasty."

"Oh, I ain't forgettin' her," Train said. "After the gold comes the woman."

***

Back at the Bighorn Saloon Sheriff Peters put his empty mug on the bar and said, "I got to get to my rounds. So you won't be goin' over to the Broken Oar?"

"I don't even know where the Broken Oar is," Clint said.

"Just a coupla blocks from the docks," Peters said. "You can't miss it, all the dock workers and river rats drink there. But right now there's five gunnies in there."

Peters left the bar.

"First he tells us not to go there," Artie said, "and then he gives you directions."

"I noticed that," Clint said.

"He wants you to go and chase them fellers outta town," Artie said.

"You're probably right."

"You gonna do that?" Artie asked.

"I don't like the idea of the sheriff sending me in to do his job," Clint answered.

"I don't blame you," Artie said. "It's his responsibility."

"And yet," Clint said, "we're probably the reason they're here."

"Don't matter," Artie said, "still his job. But if you wanna go over there, I'll back ya."

"If it was five dock workers I'd say sure, but not five gunmen," Clint said. "Those big hands of yours are no match for guns."

"You're not going over there alone, are you?"

"I'm not looking to go up against five guns," Clint told him. "I don't know how they'll follow us up the river, but there may be a way for me to pick them off, one by one."

"I hope so," Artie said.

"Of course," he added, "that depends on who their leader is, and whether or not he knows what he's doing."

"How do we find that out?" Artie asked.

"Well, I've always thought the best way to find something out," Clint said, "was to ask."

***

Sam Train put his mug down with a bang.

"Okay, enough playin' around," he said. He pointed to Johnson and Maxwell. "You two, find out where the Gunsmith is stayin'."

"How do we do that?" Maxwell asked.

"Check all the hotels."

"All of 'em?" Johnson asked.

"How many can there be in this town?" Train asked. "Go!"

The two men left their beer mugs on the bar and walked out of the now empty saloon.

"And what do we do?" Cardwell asked, while Hastings listened.

"You men get on the street and see what you can find out."

"About what?" Hastings asked.

"About Clint Adams. About the gold. Any of that."

"And how do we find that stuff out?" Cardwell asked.

"You keep your ears open," Train said, "and if you hear something interestin', ask some questions."

"And what if we run into the Gunsmith?" Hastings asked.

"You wanna try him?" Train asked.

"Hell, no!"

"Then don't run into him. And while you're at it, stay away from the local law."

"We ain't afraid of the law," Hastings said as the two men stood up.

"I ain't sayin' be afraid, I'm sayin' stay away from him, ya got it?"

"We got it," Cardwell said.

"Then get out," Train said, "I need time to think."

"Um speakin' of the law," Cardwell said.

"Yeah?"

"You think word's gonna get out that we emptied this place?"

"This dump? Why would it?"

Cardwell shrugged. If Train wasn't worried about it, he wasn't. He and Hastings left the dump.

Chapter Thirty-Six

"You're gonna do what?" Artie asked.

"Go to the Broken Oar."

"You told the sheriff you wouldn't go."

"I changed my mind."

"Why?" Artie asked. "One beer too many? Now you're ready to face five guns?"

"No," Clint said. "I'll see how many are there. Maybe I can catch one of the men alone and question him. Maybe even the leader."

"We don't know who the leader is," Artie said.

"The sheriff might."

"You gonna ask him?"

"Sure," Clint said. "Just out of curiosity."

"You think he'll tell you?"

"Why not?"

Artie put his mug down.

"Why didn't he tell us before, then?" he asked.

Clint put his mug on the bar.

"Because we didn't ask him."

***

Artie offered to go along, but instead Clint suggested he go back to the hotel and stay there.

"I'll let you know what I find out."

"Okay, but watch your back."

"I always do."

As Artie headed for the hotel, Clint went to the sheriff's office. He found the man wiping off his desk with a cloth.

"Spill something?" Clint asked.

"I'm dustin'," Peters sad. "Gotta keep the place clean." He put the cloth down. "What can I do for you?"

"You mentioned five men riding into town," Clint said. "You didn't mention if you knew them or not."

"No, I didn't," Peters said. "Actually, I only know one of them."

"The leader?"

"That's right."

"Care to tell me his name?"

"It's Sam Train."

"I know that name," Clint said. "I've seen it on some wanted posters."

"Not around here," Peters said. "I checked."

"I see."

"But that doesn't mean I like havin' him here," Peters said. "or you. And sure as hell not the two of you at the same time."

"Can't say I blame you for that."

"You still leavin' in the mornin'?" the lawman asked.

"First thing."

"Try stayin' out of trouble til then, will you?"

"I'll give it my best shot," Clint promised.

***

When the knock came at her door Fiona opened it with a smile.

"What took you so long?" she asked.

"I had things to do with Clint," Artie said, entering. He closed the door behind him, and hurriedly shed his clothes.

Fiona took him in. He was a huge man, in every way. His cock and balls dangled heavily. He was not as skilled a lover as Clint, but he made up for it in other ways.

"What's Clint gonna say when he finds out we been fuckin'?" Artie asked.

"He won't," Fiona said, peeling off her clothes. "This will stay our little secret."

He reached for her, picked her up, letting her sit in his hands, and carried her to the bed.

"He don't know what he's missin', does he?" he asked.

"No," Fiona lied, "he doesn't."

***

Now that he knew who he was dealing with, the kind of man he was, Clint walked over to the Broken Oar. As he suspected, Sam Train was alone. This man did not keep others around him to shield him. But he also didn't allow others around him who might try to kill him. That was why he had taken over the Broken Oar, and forced everyone out.

Clint went through the batwing doors, and stopped.

"I've been expectin' you," Train said.

Clint looked around.

"Don't worry," Sam Train said. "We're alone. Oh, except for the bartender. Would you like a beer?"

"Yes," Clint said.

"Then come on, have a seat. Bartender, a beer for the Gunsmith."

As Clint walked to the table, still alert for an ambush, the bartender came over with a beer, and nothing else.

"Thanks," Clint said, sitting across from Train. The man was in his 40's and looked to have been through many battles. His face was scarred, as were his hands.

"We're both here for the same thing, Adams," Train said. "Gold."

"So?"

"I say we go and get it together."

"You and yours, me and mine?" Clint asked.

"No," Train said, pausing to drink some beer. "Just you and me. Fifty-fifty split."

"Do you know where it is?"

"No," Train said. "Do you?"

"No."

"But one of you knows?"

"No."

Train frowned.

"You're lyin'."

"I'm not."

Sam Train drank again, taking the time to think things over.

"But you're gonna figure it out, ain't ya?" he said, finally. "You and those other two? They know what Eddie Lee knew."

"Don't *you* know?" Clint asked. "Didn't he tell you before you killed him?"

Sam Train made a face like he had just tasted something bad.

"One of my men killed him before he could talk," Train admitted.

"Well," Clint said. "That was a mistake."

"Yeah, it was," Train said. "But your people, they both knew him."

"Did they?"

"Didn't they?"

Clint shrugged.

"So we don't have a deal?" Train asked.

"We don't," Clint said.

"So I should have my men kill you."

"Or do it yourself," Clint said, and then added, "If you can."

Train studied Clint for a few moments.

"I don't know if I can or not," Train said. "But it's not gonna happen, yet."

"When, then?"

"After you and your people find all that gold," Train said, with a smile. "Then we'll kill the three of you, and take it for ourselves."

"You mean, you'll try."

Train waved at the bartender.

"Two more beers!"

Chapter Thirty-Seven

As Clint walked down the hall to his hotel room he heard a great roar, and then a scream. He was passing Fiona's room at the time. He pressed his ear to the door, heard grunts and groans, and smiled.

Good for Artie.

He continued on to his room . . .

***

Fiona rode Artie's huge, cock up and down as hard as she could, and couldn't help but scream with his upward thrusts met hers. He was the largest man she had ever had inside of her. After he roared and she screamed, the grunting became quiet as they both strained from the effort. For a moment, she thought she heard the floor-boards in the hall creak. Then, when she heard them again, she smiled and went back to her task with renewed vigor . . .

***

Clint entered his room, hung his gunbelt on the bed-post, and sat. Since Fiona and Artie were going at it right at that moment, maybe he had a quiet, restful night to look forward to. He would need it for the journey ahead of them.

He would have killed Sam Train, but that would have muddled things. He might have had to deal with the sheriff, then, and he certainly would have had to deal with Train's men. No, any killing was better left for later. And Sam Train seemed to feel the same way.

They had finished their beer, and Clint walked out of the Broken Oar, secure that Train would not shoot him in the back. When the time came they would face each other for the gold.

Clint still had no ideas how Train and his men would follow them up the river. Once he and Artie and Fiona were on the flatboat, they ought to be able to put some distance between them—unless there was another bottleneck, this time in the Little Bighorn. He would have to check with Artie and see what Eddie Lee had told him.

Clint hoped that no one would knock on his door that night—not either of his partners, not the sheriff, and not Sam Train. And not the desk clerk with some kind of message. He wanted to be left alone.

And he was . . .

***

He woke the next morning feeling refreshed. Maybe Fiona and Artie had worn each other out last night, because she had not come down the hall looking for him. Of course, she could have been expecting him to knock on her door, and she might be upset that he didn't. But while he wasn't upset that Artie slept with her—or had been doing it all along—he didn't like the idea of being on any woman's string. So Fiona could spend as much time with Artie as she wanted to. Clint was done.

He dressed and, with his saddlebags over his shoulder and rifle in hand, knocked on Artie's door. When his friend answered it he looked a little worse for wear.

"Wow," Clint said, "rough night?"

"Don't ask," Artie answered. "I just wanna eat and get goin'."

They walked down the hall and knocked on Fiona's door. There was no answer. Clint knocked again, then looked at Artie.

"Something might be wrong," he said. "You mind? You've got a bigger shoulder."

"No problem."

Artie took two steps back, then plowed into the door, slamming it open.

They entered the room and looked around. It was empty. Fiona wasn't there, and what few personal effects she had were also gone.

"What the hell—" Clint said, looking at Artie.

"Whataya askin' me for?"

"You were with her last night," Clint pointed out.

"What? Whataya mean—"

"Come on, Artie," Clint said. "I heard you all the way down the hall."

"Hey, it was her idea," Artie said. "I was just—"

"Look," Clint said, "it doesn't matter that we were both sleeping with her."

"You, too?"

"Forget about that for now," Clint insisted. "Did she say anything last night about leaving early?"

"No," Artie said, "she said she was having breakfast with us."

"Then maybe we'll find her down the street," Clint said.

They went down to the lobby and at the last minute Clint decided to ask the clerk if he saw Fiona leave.

"Well . . ." the young man said.

"Well what?"

"She, uh, checked out."

"When?"

"About two hours ago."

"At six a.m.?"

The clerk nodded.

"And did she say where she was going?"

"No, sir."

Clint looked at Artie, who shrugged, and then Clint said, "The boat."

Chapter Thirty-Eight

The boat was gone.

"That bitch!" Artie shouted.

"I wonder if this was her plan all along," Clint said. "To come this far and then leave us behind."

"Fuck us in more ways than one," Artie said.

"Exactly."

"But . . . by herself?" Artie said.

"I doubt it," Clint said. "She could have grabbed a couple of these men around here, or . . . Oh, Jesus."

"What?"

"Or Sam Train," Clint said. "I was wondering how he knew to come here."

"You think she was workin' with Train?"

"Yes, I think she might be."

"So what do we do?"

"You ask around here if anyone saw her leave, and who with," Clint said.

"And you?"

"I'm going to see if I can find Sam Train. If not, I'll talk to the sheriff and see what he knows."

"And what about eatin'?"

Clint waved a hand.

"Eat what you want when you want, Artie," he said. "Just get us the information."

"Right."

"There's still the possibility she was taken against her will."

"Do you really think Fiona can be made to do anythin' against her will?" Artie asked.

"Probably not," Clint said. "I'll meet you here in about an hour."

***

The only place Clint could think to look for Sam Train was the Broken Oar, but the doors were closed and locked. Would Train have gotten a hotel room? Or slept in the saloon? The sheriff would probably know.

He didn't find the lawman in his office, but walking the streets, doing his early morning rounds.

"I thought you'd be leaving this morning," Peters said.

"I was," Clint said. "Turns out one of my party had other plans."

"The big fella?"

Clint shook his head.

"Fiona."

"Ah."

"She left with the boat," Clint said. "What I don't know is whether or not she went of her own will. Or who with."

"And who are you thinking?"

"Train, maybe."

"Have you looked for him?"

"I don't know what hotel he's in," Clint said, "or if he even got a hotel room."

"He did," Peters said. "He and his men. Why don't I walk over there with you and find out?"

"Suits me," Clint said.

***

Sheriff Peters led Clint over to the River Run Hotel.

"I know he and his men got three rooms here," he said. "He probably got one for himself, and made the others share."

They entered the lobby and approached the front desk, where a wizened old clerk stared at them.

"Sam Train, Ezekial," Peters said. "Has he checked out?"

"He didn't check out," the clerk said, "but he left, without payin' his bill."

"When did he leave?" Clint asked.

"Early this morning."

"And his men?"

"Two went with him," the clerk said. "Two are still in their room."

"What room?" Peters asked.

"Five."

"Was there a woman here for them?" Clint asked.

"No," Ezekial said, "but I did hear the leader talk about meeting a woman at the docks."

Clint and Peters moved back from the desk.

"Looks like your lady might've left you, and Train left two of his men behind."

"Let's see what they know," Clint said. "Maybe they're supposed to meet him someplace with their horses."

"Good point," Peters said.

They went up the stairs to the second floor and pounded on the door of room 5. When one of the men opened it, they pushed their way in.

"I'm Sheriff Peters," the lawman said.

"What the hell—" the man in the bed said, staring at them.

The other man was still on his feet, still wearing a shirt he had slept in.

"I need your names," Peters said.

"Hastings," the man in the bed said.

"Cardwell," the other man said. "What's goin' on?"

"You tell us," Clint said. "It looks like your boss, Train, has lit out with his other two men, and a woman who I thought was working with me."

"Fiona," Hastings said.

"Yes, that's right."

"You know her?" Peters asked.

"She's Train's girl," Cardwell said. "And Whataya mean he lit out?"

"She's gone," Clint said, "my flatboat is gone, Train's gone, and so are the other two men."

"Johnson and Maxwell," Hastings said. "They're gone?"

"That's what the desk clerk said," Peters responded. "They checked out early this morning."

"T-that can't be," Cardwell said. "Why would they leave us?"

"Did they leave you?" Clint asked.

"Whataya mean?" Cardwell asked.

"Well, you probably wouldn't have fit on the flatboat," Clint said. "So maybe you're supposed to take the horses and meet them."

"Meet 'em where?" Hastings asked, scratching his head and then yawning.

"Upriver, maybe," Clint said.

"Upriver where?" Cardwell asked. "We don't know where the gold is, so how can we meet him there?"

"Why don't we go to my office and talk about it?" Peters suggested.

"Are we under arrest?" Hastings asked.

"Not right now," Peters said.

"Then why should we go with you?" Cardwell asked. "We ain't done nothin'."

"We thought you might want to help us find your boss," Clint said. "After all, he left you behind, didn't he?"

"Yeah," Hastings said, "yeah, he did."

"Besides," Peters asked, "do you two have money to pay for the three rooms?"

"Huh?" Cardwell said.

Chapter Thirty-Nine

While the sheriff took the two men to his office, Clint went back to the docks to meet with Artie and tell him what he found out.

"Why's the sheriff gettin' involved?" Artie asked.

"I think because he wants us to leave town."

"And how are we supposed to do that?" Artie asked. "Even if we rent horses, where do we go?"

"We've got to go upriver," Clint said, "after Train, Fiona and those other two."

"Do you think Fiona knows where to find the gold?" Artie asked.

"No more than you do," Clint said. "She might know what Eddie Lee told her, and you."

"That it can only be spotted from the river," Artie said. "So how do we get upriver?"

"We get another boat," Clint said.

"Where are we gonna get another boat?"

Clint pointed. Artie turned to look, saw that the steamboat Sunny Jim was still at the dock.

***

"Where's the captain?" Clint called up to a crewman.

"He's on shore."

"When are you shoving off?"

"He should be back any minute," the man said. "The pilot's ready to go."

Clint turned to Artie.

"I'll stay and wait for the captain," he said. "You go and see if the sheriff's found out anything. Also, see if he can hold those two for a while."

"What for?"

"Just in case they weren't left behind," Clint said. "If they're going to meet Train somewhere with their horses, I'd like the sheriff to hold them up for a while."

"Okay. Then what?"

"Get the hell back here so we don't leave without you."

"You really think the captain will take us?"

"Oh, he'll take us," Clint said, "but we're going to have to give him Fiona's cut of the gold."

"Well, why not?" Artie said. "It doesn't cost us anythin' extra."

"Get going," Clint said, "and get right back here."

"What about supplies?"

"I'm sure the captain has plenty," Clint said.

Artie turned and hurried away.

***

"Adams!"

Clint looked around to see who was calling his name. Finally, he looked up and saw the pilot, Danny.

"Danny, isn't it?" he asked.

"That's right," Danny said. "I hear you're lookin' for the captain."

"That's right, I am."

"I saw your girl leave on the flatboat this morning," Danny said. "She had three other men with her."

"That's what I understand."

"Looks like she ran out on you."

"Looks like it."

"So I assume you want to take the captain up on his offer?" the pilot asked.

"I think I have to," Clint said. "We need a ride."

"The captain hasn't been around this mornin'," Danny said, "so if I was you, I'd make my deal with him before he finds out your girl ran out on you."

"So you're not going to tell him?"

"Not me," Danny said. "Let the old goat find out for himself."

"Thanks."

"I gotta go," the pilot said. "Here he comes."

Clint turned, saw the captain walking up the dock toward him.

"Well," Captain James Sinclair said. "I'm not sure I expected to see you this morning."

"Not sure I did, either," Clint said, "but we've decided to take you up on your offer, if it still stands."

"My offer?" Sinclair said. "Remind me what that was."

"A ride up the Little Bighorn River," Clint said.

"And?"

"And a split of the gold," Clint said, "if we find it."

"A fifty-fifty split?" the captain asked.

"I can't agree to that," Clint said. "It'll be more like twenty-five percent."

"Well," Sinclair said, "since there are three of you, I suppose that's fair. So get onboard."

Clint looked around, didn't see Artie.

"How long do we have?" Clint asked.

"As long as it takes me to get onboard, make my way to the pilot house, and then have the gangplank pulled up. Good luck."

The captain went up the gangplank and Clint wondered, if Artie didn't show up, if he should leave without him. It was the big man who got him involved in the whole thing, so what would be the point of going on without him? Clint had no idea where the gold might be.

So he waited.

A man stuck his head out and said, "Hey, we're gettin' ready to pull the gangplank in."

"I need another couple of minutes," Clint said.

"That's about all you've got."

Clint went over and stepped up onto the bottom of the gangplank. He figured they couldn't pull it in if he was standing on it.

And then he saw him. The big man was walking up the dock.

Clint moved further up the gangplank, hoping Artie could see him, and he waved.

"Run!" he shouted.

Artie ran—or lumbered—and got to the bottom of the gangplank as Clint got to the top.

"Come on, big guy!" he shouted. "They're getting ready to shove off."

Breathlessly, Artie rushed up the gangplank, and then two men grabbed it and pulled it up.

"You made it," Clint said.

"So I guess we have a deal," Artie said.

"We do," Clint said. "Twenty-five percent."

"That's good, right?"

Considering Fiona would have gotten a third, that was very good.

Chapter Forty

Clint and Artie made their way up to the pilothouse, where the captain was standing behind his pilot, Danny.

"We're off," Sinclair said. "I'm going to have someone show you to your cabin. I'm afraid you'll have to share one."

"That's fine."

"No problem with the lady?" the captain asked.

"Unfortunately," Clint said, "the lady didn't make it."

"We left without her?" the captain asked, surprised.

"The other way around," Clint said. "She left without us."

Now the captain looked very surprised.

"So she ran out on you," he said.

"More like rowed out on us," Clint said. "She took the flatboat and left with a fella who was apparently her man."

"Just the two of them?"

"There are four of them on the boat."

"And you're hoping we can catch up to them?" Sinclair asked.

"Exactly."

"So you're cutting me in for her percentage."

"Exactly," Clint said.

"Barring the possibility, of course, that she gets to the gold first."

"Right again."

"Well," Sinclair said, "to tell you the truth I don't have a problem with being second choice."

"Then we don't have a problem," Clint said.

"Not at all," Sinclair said. "We'll be on the lookout for the flatboat, whether it's on the river, or on shore."

"Good."

"And what about the gold?" Sinclair asked. "I'm sure there's something you know about the location?"

Clint looked at Artie.

"There is somethin' that my source told me to look for," Artie said.

"And what's that?" the captain asked, cheerily.

"I think I ought to stay up here and watch for it, myself," Artie said. "Then I can point it out to your pilot."

"That's very careful of you," Sinclair said, then looked at Clint. "And you? Would you like to see our guest cabin?"

"I think I'll be fine up here with Artie and your pilot," Clint said.

Captain Sinclair smiled.

"You're both very careful men, aren't you?"

"Well," Clint said, "if that was true Artie and I would be on a flatboat, right now, and not here chasing one."

"That's true enough. Well, I've got cargo to check and forms to fill out. I'll send another man in, and if you spot anything, you can send him to fetch me."

"We'll do that," Clint said.

"Yes, well," Sinclair said, "Danny will make sure you do that, right Danny?"

"Aye, sir."

"Until later, gentlemen."

The captain left the pilothouse. Moments later a crewman came in, stood just inside the door with his massive arms folded.

"Gents, this is Harry Bilko," Danny said, "although the rest of the crew calls him Ham Hands Harry, for obvious reasons."

Harry held his hands out to illustrate the reason. And since they were at the end of those massive arms, they were huge. He then folded his arms, again.

"Nice to meet you, Harry," Artie said, sizing the man up and down.

Clint knew Artie hadn't met many men who could match him in size. He thought Artie was a little bigger, but he wouldn't have wanted to put money on it.

Chapter Forty-One

Clint and Artie kept a sharp eye out on the river ahead of them.

"How far could they have gotten?" Clint asked Danny. "They're using poles."

"Are they experienced men?" Danny asked.

I don't know," Clint said. "I suspect their leader isn't, but I don't know about the other two."

"You may not believe this," Danny said, "since you were clearly strugglin', but experienced hands can make pretty good time on a flatboat."

"So they could already be going up the Little Bighorn," Clint said.

"That's possible," Danny said.

"And this boat? Can it go up the Little Bighorn?"

"It can, and it has, with me at the wheel."

"How wide is the river?"

"It's pretty wide," Danny said, "even if it's called the *Little Bighorn*."

"Can an ambush be set up from either side of the river?" Clint asked. "Or both?"

"With rifles? Sure."

"Where?"

"Anywhere," Danny said.

"Are there places more likely than others?" Clint asked.

"In case you're worried," Danny said, "nobody can sink this boat with rifle fire."

"That's good to know," Artie said.

Danny looked at him.

"You knew that about your boat, right?"

"Whataya mean?" Artie asked.

"Nobody can sink a flatboat with rifle fire. There are no sides to make holes in, and water would just run off. And with its flat bottom it won't even capsize."

"That would've been good to know while we were on it," Artie said.

"Is there a way we can sink them?" Clint asked.

"There's one," Danny said.

"How's that?"

Danny looked at him.

"We can ram 'em," he said.

"There's an idea," Clint commented.

"But we gotta find 'em, first," Danny added.

***

"There," Danny said, some time later. "Up ahead on the right."

"What am I looking at?" Clint asked.

"The mouth of the Little Bighorn," Danny said. "Captain should be up soon. He likes to be here when we switch over."

"Why's that?" Artie asked.

"It's not as easy as choosing to change trails when you're on a horse," Danny said. "Captain Sinclair will make the change himself."

"He doesn't trust you?" Clint asked.

"He trusts me more than anybody else on this boat," Danny said. "He just likes to do it, himself."

"Oh," Clint said, not pursuing it because he didn't want to cause trouble. Danny seemed to respect his captain, even if he didn't like him. Back at the dock he had called him an "old goat." Clint didn't think that was an affectionate term, no matter how you looked at it.

Just as Danny had predicted, Captain Sinclair appeared as they approached the mouth of the river.

"All yours, sir," Danny said, backing away from the wheel.

"Time to make the change," Sinclair told Clint and Artie, taking the wheel. "Watch."

It occurred to Clint that the mouth of the Little Bighorn River was narrow enough for an ambush, but presumably the people who would ambush them were somewhere ahead.

Captain Sinclair maneuvered the Sunny Jim through the mouth into the Little Bighorn, and then turned the wheel back over to Danny, the pilot. The two men stood with their heads together for a few minutes, the captain possibly passing on orders.

"We're gonna have to start watching the shoreline," Artie said to Clint.

"Eddie Lee didn't tell you which shoreline the gold was buried on?"

"No," Artie said, "he just said something about trees."

"What about the trees?"

"He talked about Rocky Mountain Juniper trees in bunches, but with Yarrow at the base. You know what the hell Yarrow is?"

"It's a white plant the Indians have used for medicine, and sometimes to make tea."

"I didn't know Indians drank tea," Artie said.

"That's not the important part of this, Artie," Clint said. "We just have to find a grouping of Junipers with Yarrow at the base. How the hell do we see that from here?"

"I don't know," Artie said.

"And did Eddie Lee tell Fiona about it?"

"I don't know that, either."

"Did she sleep with him?" Clint asked.

"I don't—"

"Yeah, you don't know," Clint said, "but it's a safe bet, considering she slept with us, right?"

"Right."

"But did he talk to her?" Clint asked. "For that matter, did you talk to her?"

"Huh?"

"You didn't tell her about the trees that mark the place, did you?"

'No," Artie said, then added, "I don't think so."

"What do you mean, you don't think so?"

"Well . . . I didn't always know what I was sayin', if you know what I mean."

"Yeah," Clint said, "unfortunately, I do know what you mean."

Chapter Forty-Two

"There!" Artie shouted, pointing.

Clint and Captain Sinclair moved to his side of the pilothouse.

"See it?"

"They grounded the flatboat," Sinclair said.

"Will they be able to get it back in the water?" Clint asked.

"If there are enough of them, yes," Sinclair said. "But they'll have to push hard. I would have done it a different way."

"How?" Clint asked.

"Get close, then wade in," Sinclair said.

"There are the trees, see 'em?" Artie said, pointing again.

"Are you sure?" Clint asked.

"That's the shape Eddie was tellin' me about."

"And I guess you told Fiona," Clint said. "Or he did."

"I guess," Artie muttered.

"Okay," Clint said to the captain, "we have to go ashore."

"We can't get too close, or we'll go around," Sinclair said. "But we have a smaller boat that can take you in close so you can wade in."

"Let's do it."

"Do you want any of my men to go with you?"

"No," Clint said, "we'll handle it. Come on, Artie."

"Harry will take you down," Sinclair said, waving to Ham Hands Harry.

Harry left the pilothouse, followed by Artie. Clint hung back a moment.

"How much does Harry know?" he asked Sinclair.

"Just what I tell him," the captain said, "and right now all he knows is that he's to get you to shore."

"Okay."

Clint went out the door after Harry and Artie.

***

Harry rowed the boat as close as he could and then said, "You gotta wade in from here."

"Fine," Clint said, having done it once before.

He took his gunbelt off and held it over his head as he slipped into the water. Artie did the same with the rifle Clint had given him. Artie said he was just more comfortable with a long gun.

"When you want to be picked up," Harry called out to them, "just stand on shore and wave."

"Got it!" Clint said, wishing they hadn't yelled. Somebody might have heard them, and been warned.

"How far in did they bury it?" Clint asked Artie, when they reached shore.

"I ain't sure."

"Then we'll have to keep quiet," Clint said. "If it's close, they might hear us."

"Right."

"Let's go."

Clint took the lead, walking first over to where the flatboat had been grounded. There was nothing left on it but the oars and poles.

"This way," Clint said, now able to detect a trail. "Four people. They went this way." He kept his voice low.

Artie nodded, and just followed.

After walking about fifty yards Clint held his hand up to stop. Ahead of them, he heard voices. He looked at Artie, who nodded that he heard them, too.

They moved more slowly, and soon heard another sound—digging. Shovels being driven into dirt. They kept moving cautiously, and suddenly they saw four people in a clearing.

Sam Train was standing off to one side, Fiona on the other, watching the two men dig.

"Why do we got to do the diggin'?" one asked.

"Because that's why we brought you with us," Fiona said. "Keep digging!"

"Is this even the right place?" the other man asked, leaning on his shovel.

"Maybe, maybe not," Fiona said. "If it isn't, we'll just keep trying."

The first man said, "I think we should be gettin' a bigger cut."

"We'll talk about that," Train said, "after we find the gold."

Clint watched as the men went back to digging, and saw a telling glance pass between Train and Fiona. The other two weren't going to get a cut. In fact, they probably weren't going to live very long once they found the gold.

"What do we do?" Artie asked.

"We have two options," Clint said. "We can take them now or wait and see if they find the gold."

"Which do you think we should do?"

"Why not let them do the digging?" Clint asked.

"So we watch."

"Yes."

"What if they see the Sunny Jim?"

"You go back and tell the captain to take the boat around the bend and wait. Tell him we'll signal when and if we find the gold. Then come back. I'll keep watch, here."

"What if they move?"

195

"I'll have to move with them," Clint said. "I'll leave a trail."

"I ain't no tracker," Artie warned him.

Clint slapped his friend on the back.

"I'll leave a trail a blind man could follow," he promised.

Chapter Forty-Three

The two men dug until Sam Train finally called it off. Fiona had taken a walk and returned with some information.

"Come on," Train said. "There's another clearin'."

"What makes you think the gold is buried in a clearin'?" Maxwell asked.

"Are you thinkin' that vegetation grows on top of gold?" Train asked.

"I don't know the answer to that," Maxwell said, "do you?"

"No," Train said. "That's why we'll start by diggin' in clearin's. Now let's go. Bring the shovels."

***

Clint followed as they made their way through the brush to the next site where they would dig for gold. As promised, he left behind a trail that Artie would be able to follow with no trouble.

At the next site the two men started digging again, watched by Train and Fiona who, this time, stood close together. At one point, Fiona put her hand on Train's arm. He leaned in. Reading their body language, Clint figured they were definitely together—unless she was using him, too.

They had dug down about three feet by the time Clint heard Artie come up behind him.

"Is it done?" he asked.

"It is," Artie said. "If they go back to the river, they won't see the Sunny Jim."

"Good."

"Have they found anythin' yet?"

"No," Clint said, "they're digging again."

"Did they say anythin'?"

"Nothing helpful," Clint said. "It's obvious Train is in charge, and Fiona is with him. I think they plan to kill the other two when they find the gold."

"We should let them," Artie suggested. "It'll give us two less to worry about."

"You're probably right," Clint said.

They continued to watch while the two men dug.

"What if they don't find the gold?" Artie asked. "No matter how long we give them?"

"Then I think we'll have to take them," Clint said, "and start looking ourselves. Except . . ."

"Except what?"

Clint looked at Artie.

"We might have to admit that this isn't the right place."

"We haven't looked, yet," Artie said. "Remember what Eddie said about Yarrow?"

"Yeah," Clint said, "and I don't see any of it around here."

"They're in the wrong spot," Artie said, "again."

"You're right," Clint said. "We're wasting too much time. We'll have to take them."

Artie raised his rifle.

"Kill 'em?"

"Do you want to kill Fiona?" Clint asked.

"Not really," Artie admitted.

"Let's try and take them alive," Clint said, putting his hand on the barrel of the rifle Artie was holding and lowering it. "That means don't shoot unless I do. Got it?"

"Yeah, I got it."

"Okay," Clint said. "You stay here. I'm going to move around to the other side. If push comes to shove we'll have them in a crossfire."

"If we do shoot, should I go for Train first?" Artie asked.

"No," Clint said. "I'll take Train, you take the other two. And don't rush. Just take your time and make every shot count."

"Right."

Clint moved through the brush as quietly as he could. At one point he noticed Sam Train's chin go up, as if he had heard something, and he stopped moving.

"What is it?" Fiona asked.

"Something . . . maybe on the river," Train said.

"Should I go and look?" Fiona asked.

Train hesitated, then said, "Yeah, where's the harm. Just take a quick look and get back here."

She nodded and, as Clint watched, she started off on a path that would take her directly to Artie. Clint hoped that the big man was able to move out of the way.

Having Fiona gone was a good thing, though. Now Clint could concentrate on the three men. And there was no point in continuing through the brush, because even if Clint got to the other side he was no longer sure that Artie was in place for a crossfire.

He decided to simply step from the brush where he was.

"Hold it right there, boys," he said.

The two men with the shovels froze, while Sam Train simply turned his head.

"I thought I heard somethin'," the gunman said.

Suddenly, Artie stepped from the brush with his rifle, almost across from Clint. Crossfire it was.

Train looked at the big man, but then turned his head back to Clint.

"It's three against two, Gunsmith," Train said.

"And two of your men are holding shovels," Clint reminded him.

"Don't forget Fiona," Train said.

"Fiona's not wearing a gun, even if she gets back in time," Clint said.

"You're an observant man," Train said. "So, how do you wanna play this? Fifty-fifty split?"

"Fifty-fifty?" Clint asked. "There are six of us here."

Train smiled.

"Come on," he said, "what would it take for you and me to take 'em, and then find the gold."

"Hey—" Maxwell protested,

"Shut up!" Train said.

"Sorry, Train," Clint said. "No deal. I've already got a fifty-fifty partner, and he's standing right over there."

"How about if I draw and kill him first?" Train asked.

"I'll kill you before you can do that."

"Are you sure?"

"Dead sure."

"I think I'm fast enough to plug him before you can kill me," Train said.

"Well," Clint said, "let's find out."

Chapter Forty-Four

Fiona was standing at the river's edge when she heard the shots. If they found the gold, she knew Sam Train was killing Maxwell and Johnson so they wouldn't have to split with them. Of course, something could have gone wrong, but as she turned and ran back she was feeling more excited than worried.

***

Artie knew he was a big target, but he also knew he was going to have to count on Clint to get to Train before Train could kill him. He had to concentrate on the two men with the shovels, before they could toss them down and go for their guns.

He couldn't afford to watch Clint and Sam Train. He had to keep his eyes on the other two, and hope Clint was still the best.

***

Sam Train was fast, of that there was no doubt. And he was, indeed, turning toward Artie. If the Gunsmith killed him, he just wanted to take Artie Small with him.

Clint fired twice, wanting to make sure. The first shot hit Train and spun hum around so that the second shot hit him right in the chest.

Meanwhile, Artie fired his rifle four times, not rushing, and the two men in the hole fell down on top of their discarded shovels. As it turned out, they had dug their own grave.

***

Fiona came into the clearing and quickly surmised what had happened. Clint was impressed with how quickly she adjusted to the situation.

"Thank God!" she said. "I've been waiting for you to show up. They kidnapped me—"

"Save it, Fiona," Clint said, ejecting his spent shells and reloading as he walked to Sam Train's body. He holstered his gun, bent to make sure Train was dead, which he was. He tossed the man's gone into the brush.

He looked over at Artie, who had checked on the other two men, and nodded his head that they were also dead. He did the same with their guns.

"But Clint—"

He turned away from her.

"Artie?" she said.

The big man looked at her.

"We can still find the gold together," she said.

Clint saw the look on Artie's face and knew what was going to happen.

"Artie—"

"Maybe they did kidnap her, Clint," Artie said. "And we do need a third—"

"No, we don't."

"Clint—"

"I tell you what, Artie," Clint said. "I'm done. I don't see any Yarrow around here. I think we're in the wrong place, and I'm not willing to keep looking. That gold could be anywhere along this river, and I just don't have the time to invest. So if you want to join forces with Fiona and keep looking, be my guest. So like I said, I'm done."

"Artie?" Fiona said, giving the big man a look Clint knew he would never be able to resist. "What do you say? You and me, honey. Gold, more gold, and a lot of fucking."

Clint knew all she had to do was throw in a steak, and she had Artie on the hook.

He turned and headed for the river. He knew Artie was strong enough to get that flatboat into the water. He just hoped he was going to be able to talk Captain Sinclair into forgetting about the gold and dropping him at the next town. He had to make his way back to Thermopolis to pick up Eclipse.

So much for hunting treasure.

Coming August 27, 2018

THE GUNSMITH
439
Blackbeard's Gun

**For more information
visit:** www.speakingvolumes.us

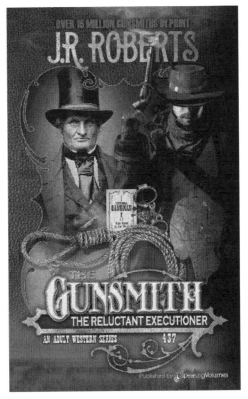

On Sale Now!

THE GUNSMITH
436

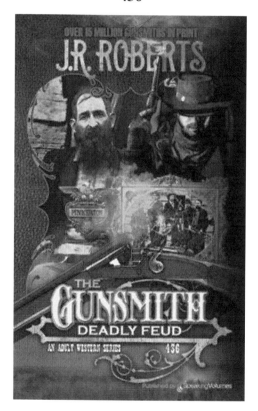

**For more information
visit:** www.speakingvolumes.us

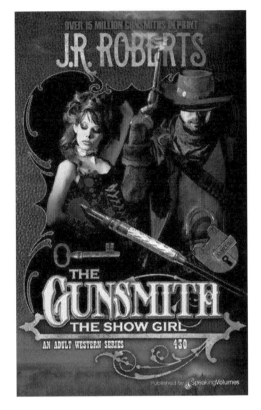

On Sale Now!

Lady Gunsmith 5
The Portrait of Gavin Doyle

**For more information
visit:** www.speakingvolumes.us

On Sale Now!

Lady Gunsmith
A New Adult Western Series
Books 1-4

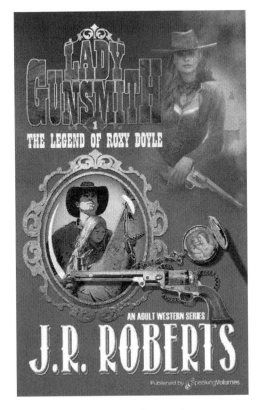

For more information
visit: www.speakingvolumes.us

On Sale Now!

ANGEL EYES *series*
by
Award-Winning Author
Robert J. Randisi (J.R. Roberts)

For more information
visit: www.speakingvolumes.us

On Sale Now!

TRACKER *series*
by
Award-Winning Author
Robert J. Randisi (J.R. Roberts)

Sign up for free and bargain books

Join the Speaking Volumes mailing list

Text

ILOVEBOOKS

to 22828 to get started.

Message and data rates may apply.

Printed in Great Britain
by Amazon

54R00130